EDOH STEPHEN OWOICHO

The Hook, Line and Sinker

First edition

This book was professionally typeset on Reedsy.
Find out more at reedsy.com

I dedicate this book to every single individual who has laboured in God's vineyard to teach His words that conveys hope to the common man.

Contents

II   Part Two

Foreword

"Everyone who drinks of the natural water will be thirsty again, but whoever drinks of the water that I will give him will never be thirsty again, The water (The Hook, Line and Sinker) that I will give him will become in him a spring of water welling up to divine life." John 4:13-14

Christ Jesus.

Preface

"The Hook, Line and Sinker" is a book inspired by the Holy Spirit, to enlighten, stir up, and transform the lost souls; for the will of the Divine, to finds expression here, on Earth. Sweet melodies from the rivers of Zion likewise, alter the journey of this edition into reality. Indeed, the Holy Spirit was all behind.

Every book has a message that differs from the others. This edition indeed passes a message of restoration to the weak, timid and wearing. Jesus Christ is the core of this book and the obvious reason the Holy Spirit initiated this book into reality.

In this edition, you'll tour through inspiring scenes and lovely melodies retrieve to you by outstanding minstrels such as Hill–Songs, Bethel Music, Jesus Culture, Charles Wesley, Anthony Evans, Ada Ehi, Sinach and the host of others. The forenamed played a considerable role in each of the twenty chapters. Rejoice, for joy comes!

Jesus Christ is the centre of human existence and the builder of every man's destiny. He is the only begotten of the Father, sent to redeem humanity from the stronghold of Satan. Without a doubt, He delights in seeing us rejoices, and that's why He pioneers this book to restore the confidence of those lost in the shuffle.

Many persons have lost their hope in existence. While some are on the brink of passing into extinction. Unfortunately, the majority of people find none to prevail as the sinker that will balance their life, and it has led many to total frustration.

Our existence prevails as a result of a grace that never fails. Every soul indeed belongs to the King of glory who reigns beyond the cognition of men. More so, our soul possesses the right to decide the reality it ought to visualise. Yet, even as we go astray because of poor decision making; God still provides us with hope to find life.

Christ is the answer to every unanswered question in existence. He was the reason for yesterday's greatness, today's splendour and tomorrow's glory. More so, He solves problems beyond our limitations.

No doubt that nothing works in motion and produces good fruits when the impacts of accurate knowledge are neglected throughout time. It is the reason the Holy Spirit is calling on you this day to pick this great edition. He wants to share with you the ideas that were never notified about in your secret place.

Recall that there is more to reading the synopsis of a book. Skip hesitating and order this book to your doorpost.

Acknowledgement

I am so grateful to God for His delightfulness, support, grace, insight, health, divine preservation and vigour to write this book.

I remain humble to my dad, Mr Reuben Edoh, and my mum, Judith Edoh, Mrs.

Also, I want to appreciate my Siblings; Collins Edoh, David Edoh, and Divine Edoh for their prayers, and supports throughout time.

I must not fail to recognize the body of Christ for their glorious support. Indeed, I wouldn't get closer to achieving my goals without their prayers and support spiritually.

My gratitude also goes to friends I met in the cave of Adullam; a place of intimacy and fraternity with entities in Zion. I'm grateful to a father in Faith and a general in God's Army, Pastor Ibitoye Marcus Segun for his prayers and wishes. He is indeed, a great person.

To my colleagues at the College of Health Science, Benue

State University, Makurdi, Nigeria, I remain grateful for your prayers and especially. Not forgotten friends such as Marvellous Iyanya, Wilson Ochugwu, Peter Iortimbir, Paul Otokpa and the hosts of others. I really appreciate your kind gesture.

I remain grateful to Words Citadel Family for the privilege bestowed on me. Indeed, it's a platform that has given hope to the broken-hearted, depressed, and those suffering from low esteem level. May the good God bless, Words Citadel Family.

Let me not leave the team those who are a direct beneficiary of my previous books. For all of you, I lack words to convey my deep sense of gratitude.

May God bless and reward all of you for your prayers. Amen!

Edoh Stephen Owoicho

Chief Executive Officer,

Words Citadel Family.

I

Part One

The Hook, Line and Sinker

1

NEW WINE

"God crushes the mountains before us simply to grant the world access to the new wine residing in our life."–Stephen Edoh.

Many persons in our world today are worthwhile because they discover their purpose and utilise it. God, in His infinite mercy, conveys us with abilities that become profitable when we work on them. Indeed, He situates in us new wine that will serve His people throughout time.

Humanity receives fresh wine from God in each season of existence. He is ever-loving for us to seek solace in trying times. Nothing is as terrific as the love of the Divine in time. Not even the love of our spouses, kids, perhaps siblings!

The words of light–our Bible admonishes us to decipher

in alpha order that no dream, ambition, perhaps pursuit makes an impact in this world when it drives outside God's framework.

Truly, He is breaking new ground in our world today. And on that ground, we are going to yield to His safe hands that will guide us into the Oasis of love. Trust will reign there without borders and constraints. Though, an intimacy with the Divine persists as the vital key to accessing this imperial locale.

One thing you must know is this: Christ wants to make us vessels unto honour. Without a doubt, we all want to shine our destiny light, become famous, and quake the nations of the world with our gifts and talents. Though, how many are willing to go through the process?

Natural Sciences made us understand that a large animal is not the same as another animal, smaller about the time taken for them to attain a metamorphic progression. For example, Fetuses takes nine months to arrive at the Earth from the womb sphere. Unlike chicks that leave its respective egg sphere after two weeks, and a few days.

Jesus Christ dispatches new wine for a radical manifestation to translate here on Earth. It will astound you to know that after a man accomplishes a mission, another man takes over. The reason is this: God always sends a new wine–an upgrade of the former to continue His project here on Earth.

No individual on Earth is the Jack of all the trade. In all honesty, nature subject humans to limitations, as they move from one tier to another in time. You might want to point out names such as Albert Einstein, Sir Isaac Newton, and the host of other nobles. Besides, I want to let you know that those men were only at the zenith of their time. Nonetheless, nature still impedes them.

Outstanding figures in our world today went through various footpaths before they become notable. When we go through the pathways of existence, our ideas attain a height in time. If we feel too inactive to go through each process in time, then we prepare to settle for mediocrity.

Frankly, there is no room for indifference and middle–class reflection in this era. God is not looking for people who settle for average. He wants to breed vibrant people in all areas of life. Affirmatively, ladies and gentlemen who will fill the new wineskin as fresh wine from Zion.

Thus, no process in time reaches softly in expression. It appears in cruelty to create tension in this journey of destiny. We must recall that even Jesus Christ took off to the old rugged cross without complaints. If a man who dies for generations in continuation kept his cool, then we can keep ours as we reach for the doorway of honour.

Our ambitions must align with our heart to defeat the beasts of this world. If the battle appears fierce, then we must recall that the journey to greatness starts with a step, and the end is phenomenal. Failure to be patient will cost us chances of a lifetime.

The kingdom is here, and it is the time to cry unto Jesus Christ to make you His vessel because a new wine has to proceed out of you. A generation awaits the mysteries God has given to you unto this time. It is not impressing to sit and watch each day pass by without discerning that a new wine resides in your insides.

There is a new power flowing in this season; striving to liberate a kingdom that will make lie down the old flames of our lives; in other to breed new wine in this time of creation. Failure to align with the Divine will create more problems than good. It will cause a generation, perhaps generations' to lose the remedies to maladies that the devil will put in place.

We need to convey the new wine out of our lives because Jesus Christ plans big for this generation and beyond. Imagine if men like John Wesley, Billy Graham, and Reinhard Bonnke has failed to win souls to God's kingdom, Hell will have added up; diminishing the numbers of people progressing to heaven.

Likewise, men such as Newton and Einstein; their inability to discern the new wine in their life will have to prolong the expiration of the surfacing maladies they conquered. All thanks to Master Jesus Christ, because those gentlemen did not fail.

If a man discerns brightly of his existence as a wineskin filled with new wine, he will live on to become a factor of celebration throughout time. Is it not outstanding each time we hear of young people doing great? Of course, everyone loves it. Besides, nobody is too old to realise the fresh and stirring wine inside of them.

Align to God in this hour, regardless of the maladies confronting you. Your purpose stands first. Though, recall that only intimacy with the Divine can pave the way for the realisation, build-up and the fulfilment of an aim.

Stay calm, for Jesus Christ is still doing well.

Inspired by the song–New Wine written by Hillsongs United.

We believe that this very chapter has blessed you. It will be an honour to receive help from you.

Stephen Edoh Ministries needs your partnership to continue to spread God's words to the nations.

We need your support. It could be a monthly help, maybe just a moment's help.

We will be glad and happy if you decide to help us.

You can send your partnership or one-time support payment through our PayPal email address below. Also, you can pay via our Cash-app username below.

You can also testify to how this book has impacted your life using the same email below.

We love and care for you.

PayPal payment email address: **Stephenedoh2000@gmail.com**

Pay Pal link: **www.Paypal.me/StephenEdoh**

Cash-App username: **£StephenEdoh**

Thank you and many blessings to you and your family.

2

EMPTY

"We can only survive against the storm, when our eyes, are all on Jesus Christ."–Stephen Edoh.

Often, we swim against the current of life; doing the needful in our every strength to survive. It is shocking to infer that not many persons withstand the odd waves of existence daily as time flies. However, we are alive because the grace of God preserved us; despite the concentration of life struggles. Indeed, His love knows no bounds, to finds expression towards humanity.

We are aware that life is a race of time and purpose. More so, the grace of God is the most vital factor every human needs to run, and stay active in this arduous but crucial race.

Because of ignorance, many hits on the pedestals to run the race alone, and that cost them the chance of a lifetime. One thing we must realise is this: the course ahead of us will only stroll unto fulfilment when we bestow Jesus Christ with the task of steering our every step.

Empty is the soul that walks alone in this realm: leaving no space for Christ in its heart. However, the soul that view Christ as it compact, and the reason for its existence delight in His warm embrace. It might amaze you to infer that all works outside of Jesus' blueprint are dead. Yet, it is the tenable truth.

Humans, in their preliminary phase of thought, cite the basis of living on their dreams, goals and yearnings. No doubt, before you came in contact with the Divine, your dreams were the core of your existence. However, that notion differs in the Sphere of light. Your being prevails, because of God's purpose, for humanity through you in this time of existence.

You'll not win a half if you kick off the race of time without communing with the Holy Spirit. For He alone gives direction that certifies success as the aftermath of our actions in the time, and seasons of life.

Your plans are the formation of choices you set in place to attain fulfilment. Yet, it is all vain work when you exemplify in the blueprint of your imaginations and not the framework of the Divine. Surprisingly, you will try to make a sense of your every action but will not find an iota of truth in it. However, this is because you never realise that Christ is the perfect truth you needed to discern.

Empty is the soul that cite its conviction in dreams and ambitions, for destruction is the certified aftermath. Note that Christ must lead your steps, else you go astray.

Christ is the sun that brightens your darkest moment. Also, He was that beautiful Star; you saw in the Dark.

Without Christ, your world would be empty: leaving it void for darkness to abides. Allow Him to fill your heart; for the light of heaven to spark into it and comfort you. Recall that failing to enable Christ to admit into your soul will only keep you swimming against the odd waves of existence.

Jesus Christ is the miracle you need: the sun you desire to show up: the living water that satisfies the taste of your longings. Give Him the chance this day to admit His ever stirring light into your most vulnerable soul, for a shift to put up with the aftermath of your actions.

Competently, Jesus Christ will not leave your most vulnerable soul, empty. Stay calm. He is still doing great things.

Inspired by the song–Empty written by Cobhams Asuquo

We believe that this very chapter has blessed you. It will be an honour to receive help from you.

Stephen Edoh Ministries needs your partnership to continue to spread God's words to the nations.

We need your support. It could be a monthly help, maybe just a moment's help.

We will be glad and happy if you decide to help us.

You can send your partnership or one-time support payment through our PayPal email address below. Also, you can pay via our Cash-app username below.

You can also testify to how this book has impacted your life using the same email below.

We love and care for you.

PayPal payment email address: Stephenedoh2000@gmail.com

Pay Pal link: www.Paypal.me/StephenEdoh

Cash-App username: £StephenEdoh

Thank you and many blessings to you and your family

3

AMAZING GRACE

"The grace of God is our only hope."–Stephen Edoh.

Grace is one valuable gift that God gave to humanity. Every human being is a product of God's grace. Each good thing we discern birth into existence by grace. No wonder the patriarch of old calls it "amazing grace."

One exciting moment, we will walk through in life is when we begin to function in the various graces of the Triune God. Nothing is elegant as His grace except for the joy of salvation.

As we continue to walk on the lane of existence, "the accuser of the brethren," tries to put us to shame. Yet, the amazing grace of our Lord Jesus Christ prevails.

On the rugged cross of Calvary, He died to make the

number side of graces available to us.

His grace is everywhere that we go in life. It knows no bounds to find expressions. Without a doubt, it is the reason true believers in Christ, excels at everything they do.

All the days of our life, we must sing His praise on every axis of the Earth. In everything that we do, the grace of God must find its expression for the Holy Spirit to certify the works of our hands.

The amazing grace of our Lord Jesus Christ is still changing lives and nations today. It is the same grace that is winning the battles that neither power nor might can win. Indeed, it is the spirit of Christ that made grace accessible to us all.

Every success story in the life of a believer transpired because of the working power of grace. It's not by hard work or skills. Recall that any dream or vision built outside God's grace constructs on sinking sand. Yes, on sinking sand!

With no qualm to this view of mine, it is the reason many people struggle to make a positive impact in our world today because they build on sinking sand.

Wise people built on the solid rock of Jesus Christ. Nothing survives a day on sinking sand.

Jesus Christ wants us to understand that He has made His grace available, and sufficient to humans of every race, tribe, and civilisation.

Divine health is a product of amazing grace. It is the fruit most followers of Jesus Christ enjoy. While the thought of deaths flows through the mind of the weak, we shouldn't be afraid of tomorrow. His grace is our compact guide throughout the series of life.

The hand of Jehovah is at work in our lives. And we must realise this truth because we are His instruments modelled for transcendental impacts. While the Spirit of Yahweh walks through our heart, we must embrace the grace of He that was, is, and to come.

Everywhere we go, and in every positive thing we do, grace is the compact guide that oversees our way to victory. If we neglect the impact of God's grace, our life will not bear the fruits we ought to discern. And this will lead us to the state of frustration.

When we came to this world, the battle of purpose kicked off. Indeed, the weapon of our warfare isn't carnal but mighty to pull down the stronghold. Yet, the weapon only becomes effective when the grace of God is at work in our life. Else, we'll fight alone. Recall that "the battles aren't ours but the Lord."

The Holy Spirit is ever ready to reflect more of Jesus Christ to us. He is the only one that can bring us into understanding our birthright in Christ. If we align to Him, He will lead us to the path where all graces are available for effective utilisation. Recall that only intimacy with the Holy Spirit brings you closer to Christ.

Jesus Christ is calling on the weak out there to reach out to His amazing grace. Only the grace of Jesus Christ can overturn a negative situation to a positive one. It was grace that made the rejected cornerstone became the Chief cornerstone.

Accept Jesus Christ today. He is still doing wonders out there. Yes, He will change your story for good, no matter the force that tries to hinder your blessings. Stay strong!

Inspired by the song–Amazing Grace written by Hill-songs United

We believe that this very chapter has blessed you. It will be an honour to receive help from you.

Stephen Edoh Ministries needs your partnership to continue to spread God's words to the nations.

We need your support. It could be a monthly help, maybe just a moment's help.

We will be glad and happy if you decide to help us.

You can send your partnership or one-time support payment through our PayPal email address below. Also, you can pay via our Cash-app username below.

You can also testify to how this book has impacted your life using the same email below.

We love and care for you.

PayPal payment email address: Stephenedoh2000@gmail.com

Pay Pal link: www.Paypal.me/StephenEdoh

Cash-App username: £StephenEdoh

Thank you and many blessings to you and your family

4

LOVER OF OUR SOUL

"The one who cares for our soul reigns for-ever."–Stephen Edoh.

Our existence blossoms as it finds its purpose in the love of Christ. It is a fact that no individual outside God's love excels in time, except for those under the hegemony of Satan. We are alive in this time of existence because of the one who loves our soul.

While the oceans of life roll and its tempest stood high, God's love towards humanity remains intact. He will hide us in His embrace till the storms of life passed away.

Cry to the Lord for Him to receive your soul into His Haven. In His beautiful Oasis, your vulnerable soul will find rest and tranquillity. Maybe it seems mythical to your thought, but it is the whole truth.

Like the Shepherd who went about looking for his lost

sheep; Jesus Christ will not watch us get lost. He will navigate His way to the place of our drawbacks, apprehensions and worries.

We must lay our trust in Him to receive the help our soul seeks. In His cover, our vulnerable soul finds defence against the shadows of this world.

His grace is ever endless; watching and steering our every step in time. It is this same grace that let the healing streams abounds to keep us pure.

We find in Him the fountain of an abundant life that springs up within our heart; rising our request to the Celestial Sovereignty in Zion.

No matter what comes our way, we have to remain strong in our faith. At any point, you feel like giving up on life, recall that even Jesus Christ stays patient on His journey to the old rugged cross of Calvary.

The systems of this world may rise against you, but note that He is the lover of your soul. No evil will take your life. Without a doubt, challenges of all kinds will wage war against you. Victory is an assurance in the precious name of Jesus Christ.

Stay calm, irrespective of the plight confronting you. The lover of your soul is alive and aware of all you are going through in time.

Jesus Christ is going to change your story.

Inspired by the hymn–Lover of my Soul written by Charles Wesley

5

HE WILL DO IT AGAIN

"There has always been one man that consistently showed up in the odd moments of life. He is Jesus Christ."–Stephen Edoh.

Galilee was a famous city in Biblical day Israel. And from there hailed a great man known to all as "Yeshua," literally dubbed as "Jesus" in English, and the Latin lingo. Without a doubt, He was and still, a beautiful soul whose every step translates the heavenly windfalls, worthwhile to the souls of His followers.

One day, Jesus went to town in Galilee, to take the burden of the people. There He healed the sick and mended the brokenhearted. During that beautiful moment, doors to the destinies of the dwellers within opened wide. Angels likewise strolled in marching orders to align the souls of the weak and the feeble.

Hallelujah! Hallelujah!

What a great man in Jesus! He heals the sick: feed the longing: deliver the oppressed & the brokenhearted. Indeed, there is no name as beautiful as that of Jesus Christ.

The son of God came to give life in abundance to us all. He came to be a light that would lighten up the darkest of our life moments. Surprisingly, none can take the position of Jesus Christ in our life. Not even our parents, spouse, siblings, or children. It might surprise you, but that's the fact! He's irreplaceable.

In our moments of trials and tribulations, He would be there to help us. He did it for Paul and Silas. Undoubtedly, He will do it again. The issue befalling you might be sickness, remember that he healed the sick. Maybe it could be lack and want, recall that He provides, and make a way where there is no way.

Good deeds are the news of him, now and then. He is so good to neglect us in our most turbulent moment: leaving us alone to moan our predicament. Like Jabez, He is going to change our story. It doesn't matter what others say about us, but God's final say.

The one who rolled the stone away is ever alive, altering the odd-taste water into living water. While others see a stagnant pool in your life, He sees a stream of living water dwelling in you. He has done it before, and He would this time around.

He went on to the old rugged cross of Calvary for our sins, two thousand years ago. The man–Jesus suffered for a crime, me, and you were accountable to effect. It is saddening to infer that He went through pains for sins; He orchestrated not! But the good news is that "on the cross of Calvary He gave us life eternal!"

Beyond human imagination, His love for us reigns. Jesus Christ is our role model for life. His prime message to the Church is "love." Maybe you feel neglected like the poor Church rat. But believe me, Jesus stands right where you are! You might have wished frequently that your Savior comes. Competently, your deliverer is with you at that exact spot you are, currently.

Glory!!!!

The sun is rising from the East to onset a new day in your life. Christ is the sun that brightens the destiny of men. He is the light of the world: the light that shines brighter unto the perfect day. Our trust in Jesus is without borders. He's going to change your story for good.

Recall that, He has done it before. He will do it again.

Inspired by the song–He Will Do It Again written by Ada Ehi

We believe that this very chapter has blessed you. It will

be an honour to receive help from you.

Stephen Edoh Ministries needs your partnership to continue to spread God's words to the nations.

We need your support. It could be a monthly help, maybe just a moment's help.

We will be glad and happy if you decide to help us.

You can send your partnership or one-time support payment through our PayPal email address below. Also, you can pay via our Cash-app username below.

You can also testify to how this book has impacted your life using the same email below.

We love and care for you.

PayPal payment email address: Stephenedoh2000@gmail.com

Pay Pal link: www.Paypal.me/StephenEdoh

Cash-App username: £StephenEdoh

Thank you and many blessings to you and your family

6

DRY BONES ARE RISING

"In every phase of existence, He raises dry bones and breathes life into them."–Stephen Edoh.

We are in a period of existence when everything differs from the former. Many bones are indeed dead. Some are on the brink of passing into extinction. But the good news is this: our Lord and Saviour, Jesus Christ, is raising dry bones. Indeed, dry bones are rising!

The mighty power of the sovereign God is moving across borders and peripheries: causing shifting for every dry bone out there. True revival is already breaking out in homes, cities, and nations of the world. I can hear a sound of abundance of rain that would cause an extraordinary transformation for every life out there.

Our atmosphere is filled with an abundance of rain: anticipating to drop on dry bones in need of reawakening. Jesus Christ is the one to water these bones, for its beauty, strength, and worth to revert to default. I don't know what you are going through at this moment, but Jesus Christ is aware. Like the dry bones, He will breathe life into you.

No bone at the moment is too dry to rise again. It is the era of true revival. Without a doubt, there is an awakening, and none can afford to be omitted from the resurgence transpiring across every home, Church, and nation. Is there any situation baffling you?

Never allow that situation baffle you: keeping you away from the original plans of God for your life. The reason is this; God wants us to align with Him in this moment of existence for His will to actualise.

The dry bone in our lives could be unemployment. Yet, He is aware. Indeed, we can all agree that this is not a fun time in history. Many things took place: causing global unrest that brought severe pain to every individual out there. We all saw all that happened in the year–2020. The Covid–19 virus did an awful job that gave the devil access to the heart of people: lending him with the task of altering the state of unaligned individuals around the world. Still, dry bones are rising!

Do you think there is anything that can change the direction of an individual out there? Such is a dry bone in the life of that fellow. Every person out there has a dry bone, and the devil at each point tries to take advantage. Just like I earlier stated, it could be unemployment, perhaps some other malady. But the battle is all ongoing to ceases the realisation and fulfilment of purpose.

We all have a purpose that God certify in His blueprint. Many do not know this mystery, and the devil does.

Satan knows from the beginning that every individual has a purpose to fulfil. And it is the reason he went straight to attack Adam and Eve.

One shocking truth, I must review to you is this: if the devil cannot exterminate you from this Sphere, he would introduce harsh situations into your life that will deaden your living bones to keep you off purpose.

Your purpose is God's goal for humanity. Never allow the devil to keep you off it, through the surfacing maladies he introduced. It does not matter what you are going through at the moment. Competently, he will try to bring you strange and demonic ideas. Such could delve into the act of defrauding people in the cyber-world, etc. The economy is his tool. And therefore, most young people are into cybercrime because of their nation's shaky economy.

The moment you give in to the treacherous voice of Satan, he takes advantage of the chance given to him. I don't think there is any happy with all that is happening. But God is aware. He is still raising dry bones. Is there any bone dead in you? If yes, give him a chance to breathe into it.

There has been no way aside from the one presented to us, on the old rugged cross of Calvary. Undoubtedly, Jesus Christ is the way, truth, and the portal to find life. He is only one capable of raising dry bones and breathing life into them.

Stay calm and keep believing in Jesus Christ. Things are going to change for good.

Inspired by the song–Dry Bones authored by Chris Shalom

7

FIERCE

"We are never alone in the battles of existence. The love of Christ is ever with us even in our most turbulent moment."–Stephen Edoh.

The Bible made us understand that God has a plan for everyone surviving on the Earth's surface. Jeremiah, the Biblical days Prophet was one of the people God made realise of His plans and intentions. He said to the young man "before I formed you in your momma's womb, I knew you, and ordained you as a prophet to nations."

We have been conversing on God's love, and it seems like we are still far from a reach point. In all honesty, it is true because God's love is boundless to the created man's comprehension.

Each stage in existence reaches in grand style. Of course,

it pleases a man's soul when it reaches out to a new level in time. Though, each new phase comes with fresh challenges that appear cruel to the cognition of men.

Love is a dialect we must understand to attract the presence of the Divine in our life. It is God's love that renders to our heart solutions at the crossroad of existence. For every individual out there, love must be a leading attribute in their life, less they tremble to the dreadful whirlwind.

Our success is crucial to the Divine and humanity. God calls us to fulfil His purpose. However, it turns out the other way round in most cases for some persons.

There is a God who answers our cries from where the thunder and lightning reside. We can't outrun the heart tethered to our most vulnerable soul. With every profound step in place, we'll collide with the Divine Love of God like a tidal wave crashing over us.

The love of God is fierce as the inescapable hurricane; tearing through the dire atmosphere to bring us hope. His fondness has never failed or lets us down throughout our trip in time. Our Heavenly Father never relents in pursuit to give us encounters that alter shifts in our life.

Fierce love is a display of an affectionate impression and portrait of a tranquil soul throughout time. Sometimes we find ourselves in situations at the crossroad of hopelessness, and just then the love of God paves the way for sunshine. Nobody can attain a height in the apex, excluding the impact of God's fierce love.

Divine provision is one worthwhile attributes of God's love. Even while Elijah the Prophet was hiding from Jezebel in a cave, God sent him meals with the aid of Ravens. Our Father's love knows no bounds to find expression because it has no foes to wrestle within time.

If we must access God's storeroom, then we have to access His love because it is the first prerequisite to drink from the river of love that never dries out throughout seasons.

Even in the times of lack and wants, God's love prevails; reminding us that "weeping tarry for a night, but joy comes in the morning." Our journey in life can sometimes frustrate for reasons we lack knowledge about in our daily life.

Many people find it hard to relish the fierce love of God today. Unfortunately, most people weep in their longings to accesses the love of the Divine. Often, they conclude that God is deaf towards the cry of their heart, which is not correct.

The accuser of the brethren will often show up to stir up lies among the followers of Jesus Christ. It is a routine that Satan has never ceased from engaging in since the advent of the created man. One thing you must know is this: success is not a story of a man that walks alone. But one who's trip to the top was pioneered by the Holy Spirit.

We must pray at all times to stay aligned with the tune of the Holy Spirit. It is the Spirit of the Divine that gives us a perfect understanding of love, so fierce. Praying is non-negotiable in this mortal realm because the enemy walks the Earth non-stop looking for whom to devour. If there is a man who can pray in obedience to Christ, I believe that there is a God who answers without hesitating.

You must decline anything that hinders your prayer because it can stop you from relishing God's love. No doubt, the devil tries to distract us from praying in obedience to Christ. This is why we must pray at all times to awaken the unseen spiritual giant in us.

Another attribute that steers our walks to relishing the fierce love of God is patience. The patient Dog truly eats the fattest bone. If an individual lacks the feature we know as patience, such is likely to be prone to disappointment. Recall that no worthwhile dimensions in life reach softly. Patience coordinates our steps into those paths.

Sarah is one female giant in Biblical day Israel that defines patience to us in God's Word. She went through trying moments in her lifetime. Though, she overcame because patience drove their destiny convoy.

In time, patience overrules every idea into existence. It is the systems of this world that mount pressure on people to succeed, and this led many to believe that God does not love them.

No matter the situation that confronts you throughout your entire life, note that God's love for you is fierce and unravelled. Keep in mind that the act of praying in obedience to Christ will bear fruits when you stay aligned and patience for the moment of rewards.

Inspired by the Song–Fierce written by Chris Aquila

8

LIVING FOR HIM

"When God gives you strength, knowledge and understanding; it becomes certain that you will attain a greater height in existence."–Stephen Edoh.

In the onset of creation, God, in infinite His wisdom bestows the created man with dominion over the beasts of the Earth. It is crystal clear of the fact that He created man in His image and likeness. Indeed, humanity delight more in comprehending the love of the Divine.

We live in a world where therein resides a system, vaster than the viewpoint of a mere man. No doubt, the hope of an average individual is the words of light. Indeed, the Holy Bible. It is so because, through the utilising strength of God's Word, a mediocre becomes considerable in time.

For an individual to live above the systems of this world

is not an actuality to reckon on; it is every believer's advantage in time. Therefore, we do not have to bow to the systems of this world to attain a worthwhile height in height.

No matter what comes our way; we must realise that we are alive in this time of existence for God's plans to actualise.

We live in a world clouded by many voices, and our trust must find expression in the Divine. The devil will take advantage of our negligence to trust in the Divine. Afterwards, it becomes an issue except that the hands of God intervene.

The tendency of a young man to reside his trust in the Divine gives him the courage to stand still when everyone converse's about the transpiring negativities. Communing with the Divine pave the way for Daniel, the Biblical prophet, to discern a mystery. And he confessed that those individuals that know their God will be strong and will do exploits on this Sphere. What a great confession!

Hell prepares evil doctrines that govern the systems of this world. It is one reason you could find many young people under pressure to attaining a height in the hilltop.

What a life!

Everyone is alive to realise, build, and fulfil an unwrapped purpose in this moment of life. Before this moment, I believe that you centred your existence on fleshy dreams, and ambitions. Though, you have realised in this book that your presence worth more than ever felt.

Living for Jesus Christ is existing to accomplish the things He wants us to attain. Shockingly, the devil felt hurt about it, and this led him to initiate the destruction of great destinies on this Sphere. If you must realise any truth that will set you free, then I've to let it out at this moment.

"The devil will go to any extent to watch you slip off your purpose. It has been his ways from the advent of man even till this day. It is the strategy He uses to keep young men and ladies from the will of the Father. More so, in every corner of the Earth, you'll find young people into acts that are immoral in every expression."

In this exhilarating series, I said the economy is one tool Satan uses to lure the destinies of young people to the foyer of perdition. Without a doubt, he does that in a more skilful way that proves how outrageous he appears.

Maybe you are at the crossroads of drawbacks, but that's not the end. Decline to give in to the systems of this world, else you'll chase shadows at the most crucial moment of your life. There is something extraordinary about you that is driving the devil crazy, and it wouldn't let him down until he gets hold of you. Discernment will help handle every hidden issue under the sun.

Jesus Christ is ever pleased to discern that we live for Him. It is true because when we live and work according to His will, the expressions of our live bear's delightful fruits in every part of the Earth.

No matter the trials and tribulations, stay calm for Jesus Christ is aware. Live for Him alone, for your walk to be crucial, in His divine life. Recall that Heaven is our goal, and only when we live for Jesus Christ, such a goal to drive into actuality.

Inspired by the song–You I live for, written by Moses Bliss

9

A BEAUTIFUL DAY TO FLY

"There is always a time when we will laugh and rejoice. But it will fly through a toxic aura to transpires in our lives."–Stephen Edoh.

The creatures of the air engage flight networks, to arrive at their preferred destination. It is indeed the fastest means of reaching out to an individual, goal, mission. No animal on Earth today is as fast as those making uses of their feathers in the air. Not even the Cheetah! It is one reason humans consider the Perigrine Falcon as one of the fastest animals on Earth.

Above the Earth's crust, there are not many obstacles as we view on its surface. Without a doubt, it gives the beasts of the air, an advantage of free aerial movement that the creatures on the land miss out. We can now agree that the combatant Jet is the fastest media to reach out to a destination. Maybe it seems partial to those living on the land surface, right?

Waking up each new day is a great privilege from God to humanity. It is worthwhile for every individual to smile after waken up from the adventure of the other world. Only a few people find it a reality to wake up in this Sphere. It is why we must thank God for the gift of breath.

The issues of this world will continue to surface daily, as we find our breath in the Divine. We often wonder why things happen in strange ways; ignoring the fact that our existence is a product of time and grace. In time, a baby becomes a man, and also, the poor become rich.

The day is lovely for you to fly. It might prevail, rough and toxic in appearance. Note that even the Eagle soars in the most infirm cloud. I understand well you await strong in faith: knowing that the Lord is your refuge, and your fortress in whom you find rest, and shelter.

One unique reality I admire each day is how the Sun shines. It is beautiful to the soul and the mind. Jesus Christ wants us to see, feel, and enjoy every aspect of His light here on Earth. It is the reason He gives us the Sun each new day. Recall that nobody flies unto a perfect day in darkness. Winners carry such kind of flight in the day.

Maybe you feel strange at this moment, but recall that His love propels us for the dawning of a new every morning. The feelings can't be wrong if we set our gaze on the Divine. Yes, it's a beautiful day!

Encourage yourself that you want to fly; no matter the

obstacle standing in front of you. The distresses of realities will rain on your dreams: persecution will show up, but you should not gaze that direction: for Christ is your blessed assurance. It is love, so real.

Christ is the windshield that protects you from the whirlwind of Life. With Him by your side, there is no reason to worry. His grace knows no limitations to find expression. Whatever may come your way; His words will guide you through. Great and mighty are His ways. Jesus Christ is indeed the prince of peace.

Declare in this moment of your superb strength for the devil to go crazy. It does not matter if you are weak: the power of God is finding expression this day in your weakness. And you will mount up with wings as the Eagle to fly and fly.

Mountains will rise to pull you down. Though, like Zerubbabel, you will declare that every mountain before you become plain in Jesus's name. Trials and tribulations will as well show up to speedy–tune the toxic movement, but the systems will cease to function. If the Divine sovereignty in Zion stands up for you, then no entity can stop you.

No doubt, it will be nice to wave your beautiful hands in adoration above every trial; for Christ is altering a shift that will bring about transformation and progress in all phases of existence.

Jesus Christ is working on your beautiful days ahead. Stay aligned to His will and commandment. Hence, engage in the things He loved and avoid the things He hates amongst men.

Inspired by the songs: "Beautiful Day" written by Jamie Grace and "Fly" written by Sinach.

We believe that this very chapter has blessed you. It will be an honour to receive help from you.

Stephen Edoh Ministries needs your partnership to continue to spread God's words to the nations.

We need your support. It could be a monthly help, maybe just a moment's help.

We will be glad and happy if you decide to help us.

You can send your partnership or one-time support payment through our PayPal email address below. Also, you can pay via our Cash-app username below.

You can also testify to how this book has impacted your life using the same email below.

We love and care for you.

PayPal payment email address: Stephenedoh2000@gmail.com

Pay Pal link: www.Paypal.me/StephenEdoh

Cash-App username: £StephenEdoh

Thank you and many blessings to you and your family

10

HIS GRACE NEVER FAILS

"One truth I know is this: Jesus never errs."–Stephen Edoh.

We all have experiences that serve as guides to those coming up in time. Each one of us has a walk through terrible moments that break down the walls of our heart. Yet, we overcame by the grace, Jesus made available to us, on the old rugged cross of Calvary.

Every creature on Earth is a product of a grace that never fails. We often marvel at the wonders of brilliant creations that God contrives into reality. His grace is indeed unfailing and insured.

The grace of God is the reason we are alive in this time of existence; for Zion's purpose to find expression through us, here on Earth. One fact you must discern is this: nobody can overthrow the systems of this world, ignoring the influence of God's grace.

My boyhood teacher told us that God's grace never fails. In all honesty, his assertions were valid. However, only a few persons could understand his message back in boyhood.

At Golgotha, Jesus's grace made us perfect and whole before the systems of this world. It does not matter who feel sorry for our shortcomings and travails. Our trust and faith must find expression in the grace of God that never fails.

Decline to recede to the dilemmas and upheavals confronting you at the crossroad of existence. Satan using his trickiest reflection programs them to distract you daily, as the sun rises from the East. We must note that God has never ceased to function at any point in time. He is indeed time, Himself.

Whenever the systems of this world rise to remind you of your weaknesses; you should remind them of the fact that nothing is as potent as the speaking blood that made all grace available on the rugged cross. Maybe they said that poverty impoverishes you. But they forgot that Jesus became poor; for you to be rich.

Jesus Christ beautified us with His grace; granting us the resilience to function effectively, in our callings. His unfailing grace made us children of the free woman; for us to possess our divine heritage as God's children.

The grace of God is our advantage that makes the impossible becomes possible. Nobody can indeed play a half the role played by the grace of God in our lives.

Hannah came in contact with the grace of the Divine, and her story changed forever. Likewise, Sarah, the mother of nations, accessed this unfailing grace. The basis of this paragraph is to let you know that they were people in critical conditions that accessed God compassion in the Biblical days.

Character determines the state of every destiny. The way we relate to existence will tell how far, we will go in life. Recall that God gives grace to the humble, and He resists the proud.

Therefore, if we must access God's grace, we must rework on our attitudes towards the Divine, also with folks out there. Until we repent of our ills, the doorway to our inheritance stays far from a reach point. It does not matter the state of your condition at the moment. Probably, it was why you could not access your healing and breakthrough. Tell him to break you at this instant. It is because tremendous things are about happening, as we round up this series.

I am a product of the grace that never fails. Jesus Christ is alive. He is still doing good in every angle of the Earth.

Inspired by the song "He never fails" written by Detrick Haddon

11

NO CONDEMNATION

" **J**esus Christ shed His blood on the old rugged cross of Calvary, to pay the price of redemption over condemnation."–Stephen Edoh.

Satan uses the sins of the past to trap people in the dungeon of unfulfilled destines. Without a doubt, Satan has been using this system for centuries, to get hold of great potentials. Besides, he does that to individuals who don't have intimacy with Christ Jesus.

However, a time came when God became frustrated with this devilish tool, we know as condemnation. Because of His unfailing love, He sent His only son to bring us redemption that we may realise, and take part in our inheritance.

The Bible book of Romans made us realised that there is no condemnation for those in Christ Jesus. More so, the

Bible made us understand that everyone in Christ, Is a new creation, and old things pass into extinction.

To reside or be in Christ is to accept Jesus as Lord over your life: doing all His will, and commandments In every season of existence. It is the most remarkable thing that will ever happen to an individual in life. Because acknowledging Jesus Christ, as the Lord, over your life is a crucial step, to the doorway of your destiny.

When we dwell in Christ, the blood of atonement speaks for us. And the decision we make renders solutions to situations at the crossroad of life. It does not matter the race, religion, or nationality we hail from on Earth. Christ loves His followers.

Redemption was the message that Jesus Christ preached on the old rugged cross of Calvary. We know it as the greatest of all messages in the tale of humanity. He became poor for us to become rich. Such an action was a display of love, incomparable and unrivalled on Earth. I will not imagine watching the one who reigns in Heaven to drive down here. Undoubtedly, He became poor, for the doors of our destiny to open wide.

Every scene of remorse in existence ensues via condemnation.

Our Lord and Saviour, Jesus Christ, paid an unplayable price, on the old rugged cross of Calvary. At the time of that deal, He made the way, for us where there is no depth and height. Subsequently, nothing could contain His love for humanity: it was vast for the foundations of the Earth to upholds.

Maybe you at the crossroad of life, as I converse with you. Nevertheless, It is the reason I brought the words of hope for your most vulnerable soul. Words are indeed stirring and powerful. Regardless, words of Christ are superior to all.

Satan may have held you in conquest. Perhaps it could be an ongoing occurrence. However, I want to let you know that Jesus Christ has paid the redemption price. And there is no condemnation for those who discern their worth in Christ Jesus.

If you once do evil things; it is now the time to let Jesus Christ admit His Spirit into you. In His words, He made us realise His yoke is light for everyone. Redemption is His message. Unlike Satan that reminds you of the sins, you engage yourself into, in time past.

Never listen to those calling you terrible names because of your past actions. It is the former person in you. For in you is now a new creature working towards the realisation, build-up, and fulfilment of a purpose.

The blood of Jesus Christ has set you free from the domination of Satan. It is a new day to relish in the Divine life of God. Take your time daily to study the Bible. Also, pray, and give Thanksgiving to the great Monarch of the universe.

Inspired by the song "No Condemnation" written by Anthony Evans

12

JESUS IS KING

"Even amongst the mountains, some are higher than the others. So, is Jesus the King over kings."–Stephen Edoh.

We use names to identify with people, animals, places and things at all Point in time. Names are indeed reflective through character, appearance, norms and the ways of life. Everything on the Cosmos has a name humans use in identifying them throughout time.

All names are unique because they bring out the identity of a thing, a place, an animal, alongside humans living In existence. Whatever does not have a name does not exist in time. Therefore, whatever has a name is distinct before God–the creator of the universe.

Everything on the Cosmos has a name, as I earlier asserted. Though there is a name, God gave to humanity, which is greater than every other name on Earth. It is the name of Jesus Christ. Indeed, the man who died to bring us redemption.

Throughout this adventure, I have been conversing about Christ's love towards humanity. Though there is something great, I want to let out to you tonight. And I affirm that it will transform you forever.

Jesus Christ was the King that reigned yesterday; the King who is reigning today, and that King who will reign forever. Without a doubt, He was there when His Father laid out the foundations of the Earth and the other Spheres. He is indeed the Alpha and Omega: the beginning and the end.

When He spoke, the oceans' downpour furiously and the mountains trembles before His sight. His breath is an antidote of resurrection to the weak and dead bones. His voice certainly directs and gives the light in the dark paths of life.

We must understand that Jesus is not just King over believers, but the entire creation. Therefore, every individual must give Him praise and exalt His name on High for the good He has done throughout time.

Imagine your country's prime minister visiting you; I believe that you do everything in your strength to make him or her feel comfortable.

Over the fears of life, we have to rise and soar; facing the systems of this world in prayer, and we attain unprecedented victories in the name of Jesus Christ. No matter the situation you battle, note that Jesus Christ is King over it, and His words are sovereign to every circumstance.

We got told by our Sunday School teachers back in boyhood that Jesus Christ died on the cross with nails piercing through His hands. It is true because the Bible affirms their stories. Imagine, a needle passing through your palms, talk more of a huge nail. Surprisingly, it was not the nail that kept Him on the cross but love.

The love of Christ is ever alive to bring about healing, deliverance and restoration in every aspect of our life. Christ's love beautifies our existence and gives us hope throughout time. His love for us is one proof that He is King over creation. Who on Earth is worthy to die for the entire human race? None! For this reason, God has to send His beloved son for redemption to prevail over condemnation.

Never lose hope at any given point you feel lost. Because Jesus Christ is the King over every situation in existence. He can alter every state of being at His wish throughout time. If you feel lost, call on Him, for He, is the light that shines bright unto the perfect day. Are you in a state of lack and wants? He is Jireh–the great provider. He provided for the Israelites in the wilderness. Certainly, He will provide for you.

There are many things we can relish when we agree to follow Christ, and acknowledge Him as the King over kings, and Lord over–lords. It is good when we know the good things attaches to our submission. Shortly, we shall delve a little about a few of the many windfalls that follow us as we submit to the Divine sovereignty.

Light prevails wherever there is darkness. In our world today, there is only one light that shines through our dilemmas and trials. It is not the moon perhaps the sun but Christ! Wherever He is called, darkness trembles and paved the way for light to appear. Call on Him today, so that His light can reach out to your ills.

Peace detail Jesus Christ in a region that embraces Its virtues. If any man finds it difficult to reside peacefully, Christ is the answer to his puzzle. Our Saviour made us understand that His yoke is light to carry. Unlike the devil who keeps throwing problems daily in our direction.

The world is missing out on a peaceful aura because it has failed to let Christ figure out the labyrinth befalling it. In any home where the presence of Christ finds solace, promising realities finds perpetual expression therein. Therefore, if we must experience peace, then we all have to let Christ guides our step, and dwell in our innermost being.

Finally, progress is ascertained in believing that Jesus Christ is King over creation. Have you ever see anyone who follows Jesus Christ and shrink? Oh, no! Everything about Christ is progressive. They will come to delay in the journey with Christ, but there is no place for denial.

The world will surely rise to stop you as you follow Christ because anybody who works with the Divine fulfils destiny. Satan is never happy when we agree to follow Christ. Therefore, he orchestrates sicknesses of all kinds towards our direction simply to hinder us. Sometimes, if sicknesses fail, He uses another malady to confront us. Moreover, our trust and confidence are in Jesus Christ.

Agree to go through the paths of life this day. Every ill moment trains us for the battles ahead. Recall that life is a battle of time and purpose. Every phase comes with its windfalls and assaults. Therefore, we have to put Christ in our front to stand out as front liners.

Stay calm, for Christ is still doing well.

Inspired by the song "Jesus is King" written by Selah

We believe that this very chapter has blessed you. It will be an honour to receive help from you.

Stephen Edoh Ministries needs your partnership to continue to spread God's words to the nations.

We need your support. It could be a monthly help, maybe just a moment's help.

We will be glad and happy if you decide to help us.

You can send your partnership or one-time support payment through our PayPal email address below. Also, you can pay via our Cash-app username below.

You can also testify to how this book has impacted your life using the same email below.

We love and care for you.

PayPal payment email address: Stephenedoh2000@gmail.com

Pay Pal link: www.Paypal.me/StephenEdoh

Cash-App username: £StephenEdoh

Thank you and many blessings to you and your family

13

HE IS WITH YOU

"Whatever that happens to you in time does not seem new to Jesus Christ. He is aware of everything."–Stephen Edoh.

Every individual will go through the battles of this world in time. It is an inevitable reality none can evade. Sincerely, no single person on Earth has the intents to suffer and endure through struggles in time. It just occurs that we conflict the odd dilemmas of existence.

The beasts of this Earth occupy each path to the Hilltop of life. No soul indeed thrives through those paths, without bowing to the sovereigns of this Sphere. Recall that Satan and his agents are moving throughout the Earth to actualise their destructive goals.

We all want to attain greatness in time. However, the Earth systems dispute with our dreams. It is a tragic reality to withstand. Though, even in uncertainties, God still accomplishes tremendous things. He does it uniquely that the instincts of the created man cannot discern.

Jesus Christ has been around from the time God lay the foundations of the Earth and even the Galaxies. He was also there when God's breath collided with dust to become the created man. Even till this day, Jesus Christ is alive and aware of everything ongoing.

The clouds of darkness in an alliance will orchestrate diabolical scenes in our lives. But then, we must realise that Jesus Christ is with us no matter the affliction we go through in existence. More so, we will assure victory in His Holy name.

The Earth has had walks through wars and upheavals in time. And even till this day, She walks through the aisle of unrest. It is an unhappy scene that none want to glimpse through in time. Amid all these, Jesus Christ stands still; wanting to bring us peace, unity and progress.

There is a sound roaring from Heaven at the moment. It is getting louder all around, like a rushing wind breaking the silence of this time. No doubt, it is a sign that Jesus Christ Is moving through the horizons of the Earth. He is causing shifts in the lives of His genuine followers.

Like a flowing stream, He will realign our thoughts with His purposes. Every dream and vision must find profound expression in the framework of Christ. Thus, when we realise Jesus is here with us, and align ourselves to His will; our lives will bear good fruits.

The Patriarchs of old call Him the Prince of peace because of His devotion towards unity and progress. Everywhere He reaches, peace becomes the limelight of day. His words are soothing to everything in existence. So is His presence, delightful to the progress of nations.

As the storm became intense than the disciples could withstand, Jesus Christ spoke to it, and His words restore calmness amongst them. It amazes them to know that even the storms obey Master Jesus. Therefore, I want you to know that Jesus Christ is aware of the storms confronting you. And He is going to grant you victory.

In any part of the world where peace reigns, Jesus Christ is the reason behind every good thing transpiring over there. The nations of the world need His presence that brings about a real and sweet anointing piercing the kingdom of darkness.

Intimacy is a vital criterion to commune with the Divine. Often, people cannot discern that prayers work when it aligns with the Holy Spirit. Failure to bond with the Holy Spirit makes our works fruitless and barren at all phases of life.

I can sense breakthrough deep in my Spirit coming your way even in this hour. Recall that He is enthroned forever and will do anything possible to see you succeed in time.

Jesus Christ is going to supply your needs according to His riches in glory. All you need to do in this hour is to worship and praise His beautiful name.

Keep praying and clinging with the Holy Spirit. Recall that only Him can bring you into knowing Christ better. Without intimacy with Christ, the works of men stroll unto the path of drawbacks and loss.

Inspired by the song "Jesus is Here" written by Isabella Melodies.

14

THE CHANGE

"We gain a new identity in Christ Jesus, the moment, you and I submit to His Divine sovereignty."–Stephen Edoh.

Life at all phases will push us down to the oceans of tears: causing a shift in our heart that triggers trepidation in our most vulnerable soul. Every individual at a point in time sinned: giving the devil dominion over their heart and soul. Though the conquest only keeps up for a while.

Our Lord and Saviour, Jesus Christ, gave His life on the old rugged cross of Calvary, to redeem our most vulnerable soul. It was in that moment; He washed away all our shame: granting us the freedom to no longer be bound to sin. Indeed, we are all forgiven by the finished works of Christ Jesus, on the old rugged cross.

Each time we sin, our actions lend the devil with an

immense privilege to oversee our routines, and steps in the tale of existence. Sin is his identity number. So, each time we click on that number, we activate his actions into reality.

Without a doubt, it was Christ who gave us, a life that we may live externally. He transformed our destiny with the price that He paid on the old rugged cross. Old things are passing away for new realities to prevail. With no qualm to this view of mine, we aren't the same because He has changed our story to greater glory.

No matter the situation you are going through, Jesus Christ is aware of it. I'll be glad if you accept the change He offers to humanity on the old rugged cross of Calvary.

Many people at the moment could call you names. But recall that you are no longer a sinner in Christ because He has renewed your mind.

Jesus's work on the cross portrays the greatest love we've ever witnessed in the tale of humanity. It was the same love that made us walk like winners in every sphere of life. Though we may fail in our journey, yet, He still calls us His beloved.

We have a mission here on Earth to fulfil. During that moment, we came in contact with the Divine, reproach, and sorrow were never part of the things God promised to us. Life without regret is our birthright. Yet, only in Christ, we can attain such feet. The journey may seem rough, stay calm. A new dawn is about to onset soon.

Oh, they said that "you wouldn't make it to the prime phase of life." But before you give up, "recall that Jesus Christ never promises to have them walk with you in your moment of success." Life is a journey accompanied by a change. And you already take part in that tremendous change by accepting Jesus. The rest of it is glorious: a story that will erase the things of old and rewrite a new beginning.

Inspired by the song "Changed" written by Geoffrey Golden

15

YOU AND ME

"Outside of Jesus's love, there is no beauty."–Stephen Edoh.

Everyone has fought His voices throughout time. We indeed deny His beautiful voice, an earshot that meant good for us, and lose access to the voice that tells us "to run and not be afraid." Without a doubt, ignorance was all the cause of it.

The voice at all times keeps us in a state of rest: giving us the hope we seek for, in our moments of agony. It is the voice of none but our Lord, and Saviour, Jesus Christ.

His voice is calm, peaceful, and nourishing to the soul. It gives peace to the body organs: fuel to the bones, and strength to our vulnerable soul. While other's converse nothing good about you; Jesus is speaking to your glorious future. Even at this instant, He is addressing hope into your life: telling you not to give up.

Dreams exist to actualise, and not to occupy a space. It's too early to give up because of the surfacing challenges. Instead, pray for God to strengthen you for the future.

We can express love towards one another. But the love humans express isn't on the same page as Jesus's love. His love supersedes ours, in all ramifications.

The future is ever bright from eternity. It had you and Jesus. And all those beautiful colours. Well, you may not understand that "Christ in you is the hope of glory." But I want you to realise that even while you run faster than your shadow: He is right with you.

When people lose hope for humanity, there is an assurance that God would restore the lost days. But if you lose hope in God; it is over for you. No matter the situation, never give up on God. He has done it before, and He would this again.

Mistakes are part of life. But there is only one person who looks beyond our missteps, and His name is Jesus Christ. He cares more about our perfection because He took our shortcomings on the old rugged cross of Calvary. Is there anyone who can still accept you after failing them time after time? I guess not! Just Jesus Christ alone does that.

He knows you more than you know yourself. He was

there when God made the foundations of the Earth. Before you came to this world, He knows you and called you a prophet unto nations.

While you cry, He is there to console you. In your darkest moment, He was there. You might be shocked at this, but it was Jesus Christ that made you overcome the trials and tribulations you once faced.

Keep stronger and believe in Jesus Christ. Because you'll find yourself in His warm embrace, reflecting through the beautiful colours of life. And at that moment, He will make you realise that it's about both of you: not you, and some other person.

Jesus Christ is still doing good. It will yield consider you maintain a dynamic momentum.

Inspired by the song "You and me" written by Shime Ahua

16

I AM YOURS

" Jesus made us realised of our Son-ship during His death on the old rugged cross."–Stephen Edoh.

We will often battle the voice that says we are not good enough throughout time. Without a doubt, every single lie that tells us we would not amount to anything were contrived by Satan. It is true that we once worried about our worth and value. Maybe with some, it is an ongoing battle. But I came to let you know that You are His own!

In this time of existence, every individual must realise that they belong to none other than Jesus Christ. We are not just Christians, but ones with a positive difference. Each time we stride along the right path of life, our identity reflects Christ to the folks of the other religions. Well, just the right mindset put us on the destiny lane.

There is no better message than that of the cross. Our Lord and Saviour, Jesus Christ, died to display His unfailing love towards humanity. During that moment; He made us realise that we are an entity of honour and ones with the echelon tagged value. Therefore, if Jesus Christ died to bring about redemption in all aspects, why do some still feel inferior?

Here come the sayings, "I am yours, Lord Jesus Christ."

Every individual must realise at this instant, that they have a worth and value. And we can only ascertain such in Christ. It is because, in Him, we are made whole for the glorious days of revival ahead.

Even through trials and tribulations, someone is there to be your best fellas. It does not matter what people say about your situation; they are there to remind you that God created everyone in His image and likeness.

When you feel lost: He is your way maker. It might seem like you are lost already on the freeway of existence; though, He is there, even on the darkest path.

You could be in a cycle at the moment, that weakens you: leaving you vulnerable, and weary. Besides, Jesus Christ is aware. On the old rugged cross of Calvary, He gave to us life in abundance: from which we enjoy the divine strength of life. Maybe you are weak. However, the Bible asserts that let the weak say that they are strong in faith throughout the moments of pain. Indeed, we can only find strength in Christ Jesus.

I am convinced that there are many individuals out there drowning in the oceans of existence. Yet, it seems like none is there to be of excellent help to them. But the good news is this: even when we drown in the dead seas of existence, He is right where we are to deliver us from Poseidon.

Jesus Christ is the answer to yesterday's puzzle: today's maladies and tomorrow's dilemmas. He rescued Simon Peter, just before plummeting into the sea. You might be today's version of Simon Peter. Yet, just before you sink, Jesus Christ would show up to your rescue.

Worry not!

Hold on to Jesus Christ. For you are His, and He is yours. It does not matter what people say about you, but what Jesus Christ says about you.

Keep your eyes straight to the man hung on the old rugged cross.

Inspired by the song "You Say" by Lauren Daigle.

We believe that this very chapter has blessed you. It will be an honour to receive help from you.

Stephen Edoh Ministries needs your partnership to continue to spread God's words to the nations.

We need your support. It could be a monthly help, maybe just a moment's help.

We will be glad and happy if you decide to help us.

You can send your partnership or one-time support payment through our PayPal email address below. Also, you can pay via our Cash-app username below.

You can also testify to how this book has impacted your life using the same email below.

We love and care for you.

PayPal payment email address: Stephenedoh2000@gmail.com

Pay Pal link: www.Paypal.me/StephenEdoh

Cash-App username: £StephenEdoh

Thank you and many blessings to you and your family

17

RECKLESS LOVE

"He defined to us, a mystery beyond our cognition, when He died on the old rugged cross of Calvary."–Stephen Edoh.

Every single life on Earth occupies a space to maximise the preferences, they ought to visualise. It is crystal clear that challenges will often show up in the journey of life. Yet, just before we mumble a word about the prevailing malady, Jesus will make us realise that "before we took in a breath, He breathed into us, His divine life."

The path that leads to Silicon Valley isn't one shaped with gold and diamond. However, a path that encompasses the league of ugly beasts that exists. Without a doubt, it isn't a fun thing to ride on the lane leading to the portal of hidden treasure.

Nonetheless, with the overwhelming, never-ending, and reckless love of Jesus, every dream is attainable in time.

In the journey of life, there will come a moment of frustration. Recall that just the reckless love of God can pave the way for us to thrive. It is this same love that chases us down: giving us the strength to fight till we are restored in His embrace; leaving our past behind with the Beelzebub, we all know as Satan.

His love is reckless and stirring: transforming and informing: loyal and hope-giving. We can't work to earn it, perhaps find ourselves in the echelon to deserve it. Indeed, He gave himself away for us to breathe the divine-life of the Father.

While we were His foe, still the unfailing of His fought for us. During the moment, we lost our worth; He paid it all for us. Jesus Christ has been kind to us, not just today. But even before we taste the oxygen available in the atmosphere.

There is no shadow in our life, He won't light up, or a mountain, He wouldn't make a plain ground. He will make every wall before us, a staircase to the portal of our breakthrough.

Do you think that the mountains before you are too huge for Him to make plain? Recall that before Zerubbabel, the mountains became plain. Stay calm, because Jesus Christ has done it before, and He will do it again.

Jesus bestows us with a priceless and profiting love for our edification and comfort. His death was a price paid for our liberation. Indeed, we are a product of love, reckless and undeserving.

No matter how dark your path may be, Jesus Christ is the light of the world. He will light your path, and lead you to the portals of hidden treasures. The mountains, they say, you wouldn't climb isn't the issue. Surprisingly, they cannot acknowledge that the one who was, is, and to come lives on forever.

Open your heart today and admit Jesus Christ in to occupy it. Because when He occupies the nucleus of your existence, the devil wouldn't have access to your life, and He will make every mountain before you plain.

Stay calm and also maintain a dynamic momentum. Jesus Christ is still doing good day, as He did in time past.

inspired by the song "Reckless Love" written by Cory Asbury.

We believe that this very chapter has blessed you. It will be an honour to receive help from you.

Stephen Edoh Ministries needs your partnership to continue to spread God's words to the nations.

We need your support. It could be a monthly help, maybe just a moment's help.

We will be glad and happy if you decide to help us.

You can send your partnership or one-time support payment through our PayPal email address below. Also, you can pay via our Cash-app username below.

You can also testify to how this book has impacted your life using the same email below.

We love and care for you.

PayPal payment email address: **Stephenedoh2000@gmail.com**

Pay Pal link: **www.Paypal.me/StephenEdoh**

Cash-App username: **£StephenEdoh**

Thank you and many blessings to you and your family

18

HEALING WINGS

"The Healing Wings of Jesus Christ are still doing wonders, changing lives, and nations."–Stephen Edoh.

Every genuine gathering finds delight in the aura of the Divine. God's Spirit reigns wherever we acknowledge and revere Him. When souls begin to desperate for the flow of God's power; the Heavens begin to translate the will of the father in the Cosmos.

Often, as we pray in obedience; Christ's Spirit will walk through our presence: bringing about the approval of a request that was brought forth during the prayer session.

The flow of Divine in our most turbulent moment is ever real. It is the longing of a man's heart that brings about the approval of a request, like I beforehand stated.

God's power is moving everywhere to heal the desperate soul. The Spirit of the Lord is mending broken hearts: wiping out the tears of many: touching them with His healing wings.

Lift your hands while you are weak, and cry to the Holy Spirit to invade you, spontaneously. He is ever ready to give you back your lost sight if only you will rise and touch the wings of His power.

The Holy Spirit brings us closer to knowing Christ better. If we do not align with Him, we will have difficulty in utilising the power of His blood, and stripes that translate healing into our most vulnerable soul. Thus, every single soul must align with the Divine; to witness the intriguing power of the Holy Spirit.

We call Him Jehovah Rapha; for His willingness to Heal whenever the sick call upon His name. Maybe you are sick at the moment; recall that He is the balm in Gilead: the ointment that lubricates the rough segment in our life: causing healing to our most vulnerable soul.

We are children of the Triune God that erected the foundations of the Earth; building it in the blueprint of His will. He knows us before we came into existence, just as He said to Jeremiah, the Biblical Prophet. Nothing is new before the King of kings. Just align yourself to His restoring power.

In the act of worship, we uncover more of Jesus's identity

through an intimacy with the Divine. Lift your hands at this moment and praise His Holy name because He is touching lives at this moment. While in worship, try to voice out your wishes before Jehovah Rapha–our healer, for He heals even the most terrible ailment.

Your healing is closer than ever thought. It is good that you continue to commune with the Holy Spirit, for the flow of His power to immerse in your most vulnerable soul.

Our Lord and Saviour, Jesus Christ, is aware of the situation confronting you. He is the Sinker you need to prevail in the state of balance on the journey of life. Without a doubt, He is still healing many outs there: changing stories, lives, and nations. It does not matter how fierce the prevailing malady may portray itself towards you. Just know that Jesus Christ is aware. He has done it before, and He will do it again.

Stay calm. The future is brighter than ever before. Yet, only Jesus Christ can take us there. Intimacy with the Holy Spirit remains the key to uncovering more about our Lord Jesus Christ.

Inspired by the song "Healing Wings" written by Steve Crown.

19

OCEANS

"Jesus Christ is the only hope, where feet may fail."–Stephen Edoh.

We are called beyond our understanding to revolve around the deeps waters of existence. Still, only a few could discern the voice of He that sent them. It is discouraging how many folks out there wander around the wild ocean–a place where feet may fail, simply to end up a nonentity.

There is one who has called us upon the deep waters–where the great unknown, uphold! Indeed, we find in Him a great mystery that kept up driving despite all odds. It is stunning how our Faith stood intact because of His unfailing love.

Existence at all phases would throw at us, odd moments. Without a doubt, it is an actuality no individual can evade in time. Yet, even in trying moments; we will assure hope in the one who was, is, and the one to come.

In the wild oceans of Life, every individual should call on the name–Jesus: keeping their eyes above the waves. Because when oceans rise, their soul will rest in His glorious embrace.

While His grace abounds in the deepest waters; His sovereign hands would be our guide: leading us through the path where feet may fail, and the route where fear would thrive. Afterwards, we would discern that He is ours. And we are His!

More so, His spirit would lead us where our trust will be without borders: steering us to walk upon deep waters. During that moment, He would take us to the place where our feet will wander. Further, He will strengthen our faith in His presence.

Life might not be driving in the exact direction you discern. Keep calm and maintain a dynamic momentum. He that acts as the Sinker to give our Life–the Line, a balance for our faith–the Hook, to hit on the green gives us hope.

No matter the situation that befalls us; we must believe in the name of Jesus Christ and bring every issue under it; to keep our minds above the tempest.

Inspired by the song "Oceans" written by Taya Smith.

We believe that this very chapter has blessed you. It will be an honour to receive help from you.

Stephen Edoh Ministries needs your partnership to continue to spread God's words to the nations.

We need your support. It could be a monthly help, maybe just a moment's help.

We will be glad and happy if you decide to help us.

You can send your partnership or one-time support payment through our PayPal email address below. Also, you can pay via our Cash-app username below.

You can also testify to how this book has impacted your life using the same email below.

We love and care for you.

PayPal payment email address: Stephenedoh2000@gmail.com

Pay Pal link: www.Paypal.me/StephenEdoh

Cash-App username: £StephenEdoh

Thank you and many blessings to you and your family

II

Part Two

Chapters culled from books by the same author!

20

SELF REALISATION

"Life will only be fair to us the very moment we realise the essence of our existence."–**Stephen Edoh**.

We live without a doubt in a time when the essence of our existence demands a translation that will provide the world with a quantum lift. And only, until self-realization is in place, such a dream stays far, from reach. So far, we have conversed on significant facts relating to "self-realisation" in the chapters preceding. More so, we will talk about it in the advancing chapters.

Self-realization is the distinction of a single second that defines a turning point in the lifespan of an individual. It is the destiny pathway to dig up the hidden treasures of life. This pathway differs in clarity from the others track lane.

The essence of each individual's existence didn't prevail to bloom alone as a matter; an object with a mass occupying an area of land. But to redefine a turning point, as I until now stated. And in this series, I'll be conversing with you on diverse issues quintessential to the entire society.

Time is a treasured asset as we all know. Humans can't reverse or fast-forward time, for it's a constant factor of nature. There is no way a man can delve into the subject matter "potentials" leaving the essence of "time" untouched. The term 'time' governs every issue of nature; both the seen and invisible things. Remember, even the wonderful Celestial King rested on the seventh day after six days of decent deeds.

The time to plant and harvest differs in every facet of life. So is the equal as eating to grow and growing to perish. While the former is persistent, the latter is inevitable. A man can loosen up on his sofa and a query unexpectedly pops up in his head, "who are you?" he turns up pressured at that moment; understanding thoroughly that the regalia of mediocrity is about to bid him a farewell. Time provides with us the area to inquire about the essence of our existence.

We are all on the ride of time and cause as I often state. In time, the preponderance of youngsters around the world uncovers the portals of their hidden possibilities and potentials. The capacity of a child to hold up with a chronic thriving in his or her favoured tendencies paves the way for mastery.

My darling dad will continually to state that, "continuous practicing makes a way for perfection to step into the box." Yea, this is without a doubt the hidden truth.

A man that can give a perfect answer to the above question, "who are you?" is impervious at that instant. Ultimately, he will save many lives afterwards if he fulfils the demands of that question which in reference site its chief goal on his–purpose.

Discovering our essence in this mortal sphere is pivotal to providing the earth with a quantum lift that will espouse it to the section of radiant splendour.

Michael Orokpo, a well-known clergy in the nation of "Nigeria" asserted that "purpose is life." What a decent way of intriguing the essence of man's existence! It is now a subculture to always take a fraction of my treasured time to converse on the essence of "self-realization" in each piece I write. It's so startling that the numbers of people who have discovered the essence of their presence occupy solely a tenth of the world population.

We are angels on the runway of life. Our existence should stand as hope to others, as an option other than a detriment to their pricey lives.

Sir Isaac Newton and the host of other amazing scientists prevails as an asset in their generation; transcending to the present time is the effects of their efforts. Does it mean they were the only gentlemen in their generation? Not at all! They only align with their purpose to translate a high-quality difference. Today, as it is these guys, prevails as the joy of many breeds.

The works of outstanding men can't die; their good deeds continue to surface daily; proving as a competent tool to living a profitable life. For this cause, certain men have made the decision to be a hallmark in this generation and you are one remnant, the cries of Zion persevere to reach.

For this cause, optimistic dudes have to upward thrust to be a hallmark in this era and you are one remnant, the cries of Zion persevere to reach. Still, on the brilliant theme, "self-realization" I'll bring to you the stirring words of Paul Bucknell who laid a fantastic view of what the word 'self' truly detail in the Christendom. He started by asking, "Is self-realization proper for a healthy and balanced Christian life?" Learn right here about Jesus' exceptional view of self-realization.

Are you burdened by the biblical viewpoint of self-realization; the fulfilment of one's potential? Jesus did an exceptional job defining this, though it counters the world mystics. In the Sermon on the Mount, Jesus started the sermon by pointing out the benefits of the one who is poor in spirit (new 5:3.)

The moment we understand our essence, it breaks us before God's holiness. Before our wayward thoughts and actions; We come to understand that we have wronged God and emerge as most desirous to see the light of God's mercy via forgiving us via Jesus Christ. Biblical 'self-realization' allows us to stay humbly before a splendid God, seeing Him accomplish His work via our lives, leaving us with a reward for our outstanding God.

The world's standpoint of self-appropriate doesn't base on gaining a point of view of self (there are many variations) aside from proper fact as published by God's Word, for that reason trying to accomplish matters without God, similarly stripping God of His desirable honour. Rebellious satisfaction and deception are dug one layer deeper into one's soul.

I love the way Sir Paul Bucknell lay down the basis of 'self-realization' in the religious realm of the Christian life. It is noteworthy to lie down the perfect description of a subject and in doing so, the words of 'Jesus Christ' will have to take its position.

Therefore, I have to bring the stirring words of the Holy Spirit, espouse in the existence of Paul Becknell's to us all. The terrific thing you can do at this point is to stroll around with me as we progress in this adventure. There is a lot to uncover that will provide your destiny with a quantum lift.

Many humans fail not because they cannot be profitable however for their inadequacy to adhere to the impact of the subject matter we all know as 'self-realization.'

I'll be enunciating on two amazing dimensions and your coronary heart will accumulate life-changing mysteries.

Stay with me!

THE AWAITED

"God sent men from Zion to every vicinity."–**Stephen Edoh**.

Civilization has advanced through the rationale of time. And man has proven to prevail as a competent tool God uses in meeting His needs in this mortal sphere. Right from Moses time to Jesus era, the citizens of the world countries continued to anticipate their deliverer.

God sent each one of us to define a turning point in the realm of the mortals; to breeds probabilities in no actual location than this sphere. We are the angels on the runway of existence as I until now asserts. Just as the Marvel comic superheroes were in movie-Spiderman and Iron man, God chooses us to be the 'hero' of our time.

However, there is an outstanding state of affairs here, that many people, however, cannot understand. And this has grown to be the major hindrance, impeding many guys and ladies from reaching their goals. It's what I term, "The Hero On Time." Yea, I'm certain that it sounds weird to you. Yet, I'm petite, that you grant me the chance to explain this very notion.

One factor many human beings cannot recognize is that there is no hero born in the era of peace and stillness. God dispatched them at some stage in the length of sudden droughts, conflicts, and the dreadful moments the naturally occurring pandemic initiated.

It's more convenient talking than enduring the consequences of their state. Although, the delightful news is that there is commonly an emergence of a warrior in each hard situation. Solely, if we align with the reality that we are the 'expected heroes' then cling to the words of Jesus in obedience, our desires will actualise.

Nothing is as lousy as surviving via making a strive instance in this sphere. Many have journeyed to the portal of suicide because of the surfacing actualities. It shocks me when I experience others blaming them. Yet, it's easy speaking than enduring the consequences of their state. Although, the delightful information is that there is an emergence of a warrior in each challenging situation.

Moses was the pioneer of the Israelis' exodus from the hegemony of the Egyptians. Yet, he with no skill arrived whilst all was going smoothly. God tactics differ from ours. The Bible made this clear to us. Neither is His thoughts the equal with ours in clarity.

Time is one element I took a thing of my time to grant a clarification for previously on this series. It will be horrible for a man to act outside the ordinance of time. It's a catastrophe on its own. Without a doubt, Moses already flees from the region God has created him to liberate. Have you experienced anything here? He failed to recognize that he used to be the hero his human beings predicted for age.

Yet, God made him comprehend his mission in Egypt. Challenges have made many to accept the fact that there is no warrior instinct in them. God has sent you to be a hero right here on Earth and as I stated earlier, 'no hero emerges at the excellent moment of life.' Heroes are born in the situations of precarious epidemics. King Pharaoh of the then Egypt used to be Moses antagonist and additionally the enemy of God's chosen people.

Yet, Moses has a minor challenge–stammering, still, God

presents with him–a brother and a shaft.

While Aaron the brother of Moses does the verbal conversation of God, his shaft orient's emotional and sensible views of the superb King. At the most waiting moment, existence may not act fair, yet God does the fairest. He smiles at the state of our affairs because in God's palms lies the keys of deliverance and elevation.

With Aaron and the shaft, God uses Moses to liberate the Israelites out of Egypt. While it is subsisting as the just beginning of the malady dealing with you, Jesus Christ is proclaiming to that situation, "I finish with you on the cross." Moses already gave up because he was a man that stammers. Yet, God didn't reach out to Moses' words but His! Remember, in realizing your essence in this mortal realm, face every single state of affairs that comes your way.

King David, the son of Jesse, a Benjaminite was the hero that oversaw the Israelites victory against the Philippines or the "Palestinians" as we recognize in this current time. While the Palestinian's beast-Goliath was busy roaring like a hungry Lion, God used was gearing up a little boy to earn His covenanted kingdom–victory. Even the head of the Israelis monarchy-Saul fled sleep because of the scary demeanour Goliath voice and footsteps have been exhibiting.

Imagine, the entire kingdom is afraid of a beast and a teenage boy is coming to lay a hallmark of transcending victories. How interesting!

Do you recognize what befell when David greeted the King to earn his approval to face the beast? Hmm, the King gave him his armour. Unfortunately, he couldn't match it. The fact about this is that God's methods differ from the ways of man. While men suppose it's by utilizing power and mighty, God is like, oh no, it's by the Spirit!

David in no way has to use a sword to fight, perhaps a bow and arrow, yet none of these mentioned that that which God had ordered for utilization.

Coming face to face with the world strongest man was a fascinating actuality for the inexperienced Hebrew boy. David didn't just bring down Goliath with the five stones. Yet, the five stones were instrumental. However, self-realization plays a fundamental role in his victory. I firmly believe that the patriarch—Zerubbabel contrived the sayings, "before me oh you mountain, end up plain" via the courage displayed by David.

Victory doesn't reach out to us through the act of arguing or murmuring. It's come with the aid of exercising courage in each scenario also through praying in obedience to Christ. Many humans wish to be great, but they don't desire the fire of attainment to refine them. How astounding is it for a man to think of success, yet keep away from the negative occurrences of life?

This is one reason many younger people in Africa and some other part of the world go into the diabolical act of blood money; sacrificing their love ones, and most instances their lifespan, for prestige and wealth. How lousy is it!

Outstanding men such as Warren Buffett, Zig-lantern, Kenneth Copeland will be foul crying loud if they come to label their trip to prestige and wealth as a "less stress one of a kind." The challenges many human witnesses often are rewarding in giving them a quantum elevation that will outline a turning factor in their destiny.

Gold, as they say, is lovely and worthwhile. Yet, it drove through a fiery furnace to becoming what many humans out there admire and wish they possess. If gold went through the furious furnace to end up as the most precious element in mankind, how a much more the entire world assume of you? It's a pleasant time you comprehend the fact that you are the awaited hero of your generation and you have no time to go round joking with our destiny.

A JEWEL IN THE SAVANNAH.

"Each individual existence is pertinent to humanity."–**Stephen Edoh**.

The insane sets of people have overtime outraged many inno-cent folks in the past; leaving them in a very aggrieved state. Yes, sets of hooligans can abuse a man, but this doesn't take his worth and value away from him. Our worth displays our personality and essence to the world. I've conversed this with many persons in recent times and I'll do the same with you this time around, "a man who feels worthless is a living dead." So true!

Frankly inferring, it is terrifying each time I stroll down the street only to hear many humans grumble about their incapacity to produce promising results. Honestly, It's so terrible that they felt worthless. Therefore, many people, in particular, the youths of this era utilise the Internet to defraud people; constraining them of their wealth.

Maybe I feel so concerned, that will be your thought. Yet, it's not because of simple familiarity or relatedness; either through blood connection or by adoption. I feel worried because I'm a Human being like you and it hurts to watch others fall beneath the peak level. Unfortunately, our behaviour accomplishes a crucial role here.

The word "jewel" means a lot; A valuable stone, gold, beauty, a wonderful treasure, Pearl, etc. It is essential to appreciate yourself; utilising your gifts and talents, keeping the exact name you've endured to attain, etc.

God created each of us in His very own picture and likeness. We are all like God in appearance irrespective of our race, nationality, culture, etc. Though, we vary from him when we do the things that propel His presence away from us. Still, we are His, because He doesn't repudiate us each time we take a stride lower back to Him, even after going astray.

Our glorious father sees you in an unconventional approach to how others view you. While they see a one time smoker or fornicator, God is seeing a life changer and the joy of many breeds In you.

Often, those odd folks will attempt to remind you of the errors you sometimes put into action. Yet, the Bible said, your past was buried with Christ and your presence and future have emerged through the event of our saviour's resurrection.

We are a Jewel in the Savannah; a jim-dandy to the top-notch monarch of the universe, a treasured stone, an epitome of grace, the radiant of God's superb splendour, etc. It's so lousy to watch some folks settle themselves above others for a mundane reason. No man is worthy than the other in the eyes of God. All persons were equal before Him, for He made us all except biases.

The very instant, a man sees himself better than the other individual around him, such a fellow has submitted to the hegemony of Satan. I feel astounded by the story of the "world redemption." Our Lord and Saviour, Christ Jesus, forsook His role as one amongst the Godhead to carry all men into the authentic light. How interesting!

It's just like instructing Prince Harry of England to tidy the Palace square. Hmm, it sounds crazy, right? But, right here comes a man who forsook His wonderful crown to convey man the joy of Salvation. One truth is certain; the conditions we go through us at most instances can now and then define us wrongly to the world. And this has prevailed to emerge as a danger to our emotional state of being.

Today, many have been denied the "worthwhile reputation" they deserved. Many persons, often, view others in phrases of bodily appearance; hairdo, trendy outfits, etc., but these are all mundane things! A cool look is a signal of self-discipline and it deserves recognition. Yet, it shouldn't be a tool of demonizing others.

You are a unique entity. Maybe a few persons haven't spoken to you of your uniqueness, but I'm conversing with you at this instant of your essence. At a certain stage, many might have disenchanted you. However, it's no longer the end. One actuality is obvious; every disappointment is a blessing in disguise.

Yes, they don't care about you however it doesn't trade the truth that 'you are one of a kind treasure to God and a worthwhile entity to humanity.' I don't care how others see you, the one thing I reminisce about is this; 'you are a jewel in the Savannah.' You will become a gorgeous character in the tale of mankind. Just push those atypical views aside. You are not what they say about you.

You are the end product of God's utterances. And finally, you are a treasure in the eyes of Jehovah!

Culled from the Book titled "**An Evergreen World**" by **Edoh Stephen Owoicho**

We believe that this very chapter has blessed you. It will be an honour to receive help from you.

Stephen Edoh Ministries needs your partnership to continue to spread God's words to the nations.

We need your support. It could be a monthly help, maybe just a moment's help.

We will be glad and happy if you decide to help us.

You can send your partnership or one-time support payment through our PayPal email address below. Also, you can pay via our Cash-app username below.

You can also testify to how this book has impacted your life using the same email below.

We love and care for you.

PayPal payment email address: Stephenedoh2000@gmail.com

Pay Pal link: www.Paypal.me/StephenEdoh

Cash-App username: £StephenEdoh

Thank you and many blessings to you and your family

21

VISION

"Every woman or lady you have encountered in the journey of life admire the position and places of influence."—**Stephen Edoh**

Vision is an apparent snapshot of our plans, passions, aspirations, yearnings, goals, etc. I will like to recite a quote from my first book, titled: A New Dawn, " Life without vision, operate in friction." In the series of life, the essential and crucial key to explore any horizon is vision.

The word, 'Vision' could be linked to the process of constructing a foundation; which then detail the fact that the vision of every woman is the bedrock of her future. It is the lens of success that views our imagination, opens us to our aspiration, and steers us to the hallway of honour.

Often times, a lot of people say they want to be admired, famous, rich etc. But the lost key, which they still do not have access to, is vision. When you lack vision, you can't envision or dream of anything encouraging, because vision brings out the blueprint of your future as a woman of honour.

Most ladies out there are not making an impact, not because they are ungodly, or odd, no! The authentic truth is that they aren't visionary. Until a woman becomes prescient, her home remain a mundane empire. Yet, she and her husband might be rich and healthy, but still, not amplifying impact to the denizens of the Earth.

Historically speaking, the success of several distinguished intellectuals materialize via the influence of a visionary women in their life. Such nobles include, Zondervan's own Dr. Ben Carson, whose momma influence and faith triggers his dream of becoming a neurosurgeon. Also, women such as Faith Oyedepo, Becky Enenche, Judith Edoh plays an awesome role in their Husband success.

Vision is a platform that built the aspiration of every woman to the hilltop. It introduces the passion and zeal for success. Life outside vision is a life inside tension. This is the reason why a lot of ladies goes into prostitution; because they didn't have a clear sight of who they are. So, they ended up in the state of tension.

I groaned in pain the very moment I realized most ladies are living to fulfil the demand of reproduction and sexual satisfaction. But the story is beyond! God didn't ordain any intimacy from the throne room for alone the purpose of reproduction and sexual pleasure, but to translate an impactful feats in the taljhllhhe of mankind. This is the reason why most homes are blossoming; because the couples are visionary.

We have sail down this far; still we have to explore more on this series.

A GODLY HOME

"One of the top most primacies of any lady or woman is that of creating a space for a godly atmosphere in her home."—**Stephen Edoh**

Godliness is the translation of the divine spirit that legislate from the hamlet of Zion. It is the God kind of personality; the ways He love, the culture he held in awe, etc. In a time when the whirlwind of civilization seems to act hostile to the denizens of the earth, only the godly individuals stand firm!

A Lot of people used to think of the Godly sets of people as abnormal and erratic fellows with no hope, but it's not true!

Godliness is the foundation of every vision that denote the triggering power of Jesus Christ. In godliness one find peace and joy, otherwise it shows up from a different side; mundane activities, etc. Any move embarked on the backing of godliness stride on to the doorway of honour. Every vessel of honour you know of is a caption of a godly heritage.

The first goal of every female entity either in courtship or in marriage must based it target on the fact of raising a godly home. Men don't raise home, they built a house. Women are home builders! Still, they can be home destroyers as the same time. But the true fact here is this; as a woman or a lady, your first target in the future must be that of raising a godly home.

A godly home is not the same with the regular homes we do visit time after time. No! It differs. Indeed, it's a home that housed God's favour in all virtues. The Celestial present never find it route to an ungodly home for any reason. It only recognize the righteous and that of the just.

The benefits of raising a good home did not only translate for a vision that positively affect the life and wellbeing of a single family. No! It influence affect the entire universe. Dr. Benjamin Carson isn't great today because he was handsome, rich, or intelligent. No! He is, because a godly woman stood in the gap for him when he was a no-brainer . Today, the whole world celebrate both Benjamin and Sonya Carson.

When a woman decides to submit her home to Jesus, she submit a part of the nation's population to the host of heaven. Just imaging for once every woman raising godly children for the next 20yrs, you will find out that crime rate at that time will be at the point of eradication. The world will be a lovely place for everyone to live. Never forget, the influence of a godly activity spread so far like the wide fire.

Finally, God's love for the righteous can't be outclassed by anyone; even the Biblical psalmists testify in most of their melodies of God's involvement in safeguarding the righteous. Remember, others might put their trust in chariots and horses but a godly woman or lady rely on the true God. It's a high time you put up with the right decision by agreeing this very moment that you will raise a godly home not just with yourself but God.

Stay with me!

IMPACT

One of those things that make several women more unique than most men is the tale of impact."—**Stephen Edoh**

Impact is the effect that translate from the lifestyle or the personality of an entity being referred to as the encoder or the mentor to the individual in reference; the mentee or the decoder. It is the transmission of an abstract thoughts, feelings, ways of life, etc., from one person to another. The impact could neither be negative kind; changing men into monsters or a positive kind; influencing, converting and sending men and women to their place of destiny.

The lamp of every man's education shines so brightly. But that of a woman shine brighter. Every impact made by a woman transform the beings around her region. A famous quote says,

" If you educate a man, you have taught one person, but when you educate a woman, you enlighten the society." This only happens via impact!

One of the differences that makes a woman appreciable is an impact. A lot of people are out there but nobody appreciates or value them because they haven't impacted something great into the life of anyone. Until you arose to become a factor of celebration, the world wouldn't acknowledged your present on the Earth surface.

Women of honour are the very dimensions and portals of impact. As soon as an individual or team's of persons encountered a woman of huge impact, their life changes for good. You can't meet with an entity such as Kathryn Kulman and remain the same. No! This are custodians; people who legislate as kingdom remnant.

A lot of people complain about certain factors that contribute to one being impactful and the formal criterion been given is based on financial capability; riches. But this is never true. Impact is not for the rich alone. It is less for everyone to become a man and woman of impact. This is because it pays not a family alone but the entire society.

Women of impact are those who aid their husbands in raising a godly home. Remember, I earlier said something to be taken note of, " Every ungodly home is a profane dynasty ." Yeah, it is true, because when God spirit is absent from a home, a strange sprit take refuge in such a cottage. Never forget, a godly home is a citadel where Kingdom remnants are erected.

Impact define a woman as a component of honouranium when such a woman cultivate an attitude of teaching and fostering good insights into the life of several persons out there. When you come across a family whose mental and emotional state is at equilibrium, what then comes to your mind is the fascinating personality of the custodian of that home; such in reference is the mother.

Finally, a woman of impact is one who have discover her calling. Not just the fact of realizing who God have called her to be on the earth surface but to interpret the purpose of her calling to the inhabitants of the earth by solving critical problems. Women such as Maria Woodworth-Etter and Kathryn Kulman are good example of feminists who translated the rhythm of Zion on the Earth surface.

Never forget, the topmost vision of every woman desiring to be named in the hall of fame must be that of raising a godly home as well as add impact to the life of countless persons out there in the entire universe. Raising a godly home implies building an empire that will help facilitate the move of the end time revival. Impact on the other hand detail a move that will shift the lifestyle of civilization and secularism out of the Earth and positioned godliness on the throne.

Stay with me!

Culled from the book titled "**A Woman Of Honour**" authored by **Edoh Stephen Owoicho**

We believe that this very chapter has blessed you. It will be an honour to receive help from you.

Stephen Edoh Ministries needs your partnership to continue to spread God's words to the nations.

We need your support. It could be a monthly help, maybe just a moment's help.

We will be glad and happy if you decide to help us.

You can send your partnership or one-time support payment through our PayPal email address below. Also, you can pay via our Cash-app username below.

You can also testify to how this book has impacted your life using the same email below.

We love and care for you.

PayPal payment email address: Stephenedoh2000@gmail.com

Pay Pal link: www.Paypal.me/StephenEdoh

Cash-App username: £StephenEdoh

Thank you and many blessings to you and your family

22

Conclusion

C hapters and the Biblical verses backing them!

New Wine: Luke 5: 37

Empty: John 15:4-5

Amazing Grace: Ezra 9: 8-9, Act 15: 11, Romans 6: 14

Lover of Our soul: Psalm 40:2, Isaiah 53:5

He will do it again: 2 Corinthians 1:10

Dry bones are rising: Ezekiel 37

Fierce: Psalm 73: 26

Living for Him: Galatians 2: 26, Phi 1:21

A beautiful day to fly: Psalm 118:24, Isaiah 40:31

His grace never fails: Joshua 22:45

No condemnation: Romans 8:1

Jesus is King: Joshua 1:9

He is with you: Isaiah 40:31

The Changed: Esphesians 1:7

You and Me: John 17:23

I am Yours: Romans 8: 14–17

Reckless Love: Ephesians 3:19

Healing Wings: 2 Chronicles 7–10, Malachi 4:2, Isaiah 57: 18–19

Oceans: Matthew 14: 22–31

Every negative situation in existence has a solution. And Jesus Christ is the solution to all problems of life.

If we submit to His Divine sovereignty, then He will lead

us to His oasis of Love.

Edoh Stephen Owoicho

About the Author

Edoh Stephen Owoicho was born in Plateau State, Nigeria to a Benue indigent parents in the year, 1999.

He grew up in New Karu, Nasarawa State, Nigeria. For six years he has been writing poems, articles, and songs.

His first book, "A New Dawn," earn a nationwide commendation, from Nigerians and friends abroad. In 2019, he wrote his second book, "Woman of Honour, " which has turned out to be a blessing to many ladies in Africa and beyond.

Further, Stephen Edoh is a medical physiology student at the prestigious College of Health Sciences, Benue State University, Nigeria.

Likewise, He is the founder of Words Citadel Family; a spoken and written team who's goal is to stir, inspire and transform the lost and broken via the utilisation of words.

You can connect with me on:
◼ http://www.facebook.com/eastwind1999

Also by Edoh Stephen Owoicho

Fresh words from the Horizons of Zion!

A New Dawn

There is no qualm to the fact that we all desire the good things of life. Life transit in styles. However, just a few persons have maximised their existence, effectively.

Year's back, as a young lad I used to wake up each new day, asking myself questions. And one of the surprising queries that pop up in my head was this, "when is the sun going to stop shining?" Hmm, I guess those thoughts result from ignorance. But do you know till this very day, the answer never came? Yes, because it's a phenomenon on its own. A new dawn is a fresh onset glowed by joy.

Everyone wants to relish the stunning moments of life. Still, some find it inconceivable. One misstep, most people's deduces is this; discerning the negative occurrence prevailing as the will of God for their life, and it not true. The Divine Father plans greatly for His Sons and Daughters. He loves everyone equally! Without a doubt, God wants us to experience the fullness of joy.

In life, there are three major phases, every individual must journey through, to fulfil a purpose. It doesn't matter if you were born with a silver spoon. Just as the aforesaid recalls, truly, there are three phases! And here, there is: "The phase of struggle, The phase of restructuring and finally, The phase of exploit."

Truly, in this edition, you'll be delving deep into stunning mysteries that will give you a quantum lift. Also, you'll be able to scale through the phases of life. Recall that in life, you must go through various phases just as the aforementioned stated.

Though, men fail in the phases of life because they lack knowledge on how to win. This book has been put in place by God for your promotion. See it as a divine occurrence, accept it as God sent, and read it like the best literature, you dream if always.

Thank you and God bless you, as you embark on your journey to a New Dawn.

An Evergreen World

The Earth is an axis in existence that support the functionality of Living entities. It is a place to seek peace and find serenity.

Without a doubt, confrontations of various kinds has settled the Earth to Her knees. Nonetheless, the undeniable fact remains the same; our world is evergreen!

We live in a time, when the actualities surfacing, prevails lethally, than for good. Indeed, an ethical view of "an evergreen world" differs in the comprehending faculty of the many denizens.

Our world is evergreen; yes, It is true. Anyway, if I suppose, that ten persons distinguish "An Evergreen World" most of them, will discern it to a place full of treasures; golds, silvers, rubies, and pearls of every kind. However, I

would disagree with that viewpoint, because it takes more than treasures;

golds, money, etc., to make a world, evergreen!

This book is split up into four sections;

UNDERSTANDING.

Understanding is a tool to attaining a greater height in the adventures of life.

The expedition to an evergreen world is one, understanding, pioneers.

One thing, many people decline to discern, is the fact of understanding the prerogative of life struggles. It is worthwhile to infer that life struggles are one factor, a man's understanding must align with, to discern forth, a promising result.

A well-known quote asserts that "without an understanding for something, we will end up with nothing." This is true as it relates to the sensibilities of life.

Abraham was a man of understanding. He wasn't just a patriarch of age. No! He was a man, full of Wisdom. Has it meant, Abraham, relinquished God agenda, because of his wife's infertility, what would have been the result? He would have journeyed into extinction; failing to prove that he was a worthwhile entity during his stay, here on the Earth crush.

In time, many trends will reach out to you. Yet, you got no option, but to maximise your understanding of life realities.

ADAPTATION.

In natural sciences, it is understood that every living entity on Earth, once adapt to a certain state of despair. Adaptation is crucial, to surviving, the occurrences of life. Man have to blend, to fix into the network, of formal association. Also, Animals have to adapt to survive, breeds, etc. Failing to pave the way for adaptation paved the way for deprivation and the adverse occurrences of life.

Adaptation is pivotal to altering the world on the pedestals. A layman view about a radiant sphere as I earlier state is a locale inhabiting the treasures of life. More so, it is one thing to have a desire, and another to possess what your longing details, realistically.

Without a doubt, our World is striving towards an evergreen phase. Yet, only men who have the potency to drive in forbearance, altering hope, alongside love, live to bears decent fruits on this mortal sphere.

We must forbear to foresee a greater future. Forbearance, alongside alignment, plays a crucial role that drives our world to the phase of radiant splendour.

There are many pathways, that prevails horrendously, in reality. And in the course of your adventure with this book, you will come to behold the stirrings words that aids one to understand, adapt, and metamorphosed to fulfilling destiny in life.

METAMORPHOSIS.

There is no doubt that I continue to correlates with the fact that says "there are no mysteries that prevails without driving through a metamorphic pathway." Yes, this is without qualm, the obvious truth.

Growths, in Science, is viewed as an inevitable occurrence unless factors such as death, surfaces, its progressive striding cease to an instantaneous end. Metamorphosis, is unavoidable, here on Earth. In time, they say, a child becomes, a man. So, true!

Our journey in life must be progressive in one accord; providing no space for any intruder's hindrance.

Understanding life concepts pave the way for adaptation to thrives. Adaptation espouses us to the chambers of elevation. In the metamorphic pathways, men come to realise their essence, and the unravelled mysteries meant to define a turning point in their destiny.

In this adventure, you will tour through various dimensions that will reshape and redefine a more decent personality in you, that differs from the former.

Knowledge is one factor that has help civilisation to hit on the pedestal in the portal of transformation. In this adventure, you will encounter the knowledge of age, you once long to retain. Your journey to the portals of transformation will experience a shift, knowledge transpires.

Self-realisation is essential to every man and the world, in whole. In the metamorphic pathway of life, knowledge, plays a crucial role that speedy tune, the realisation of one's essence, here on Earth. If there is one thing, you have done so well, is the fact that you took a portion of your precious time to stride through this book.

There is no adventure through the pathway of knowledge that is worthless. It's a worthwhile step taken! Without a doubt, it is prerogative to affirm that knowledge is the only key that alters the state of a man.

Truly, it is no mistake, that you have on your palm, this wonderful book. Your tour will be an interesting one. Stay tuned, as I round up, this series.

ATTAINMENT.

Oftentimes, the majority of people wonder why it seems like forever, to attain a worthwhile phase in life. More so, they fail to realise that success is the resultant effect of understanding major principles that help to redefine a turning point in the tale of humanity. This is one reason I gave a concise narrative on the topic "knowledge" in the previous paragraph. In life, we must legislate attainment at each point to transpire the reality that our heart, desires.

Like I said, "only an understanding of principles or more, breeds forth the Stunning actualities, we desire to discern.

Undoubtedly, knowledge is the key to reaching out to the comfort zone of life. If we authorize knowledge to drive our convoy, there will prevail no delay in the quest to shift our world to the evergreen phase.

This book has been set in place by God for your refinement. See it as a divine occurrence, accept it as God sent and read it like the best literature, you've ever seen.

Thank, a lot and God bless you, as you embark on your journey to an Evergreen World.

Woman of Honour

There are many books in the world but amongst them, only a few are full of mysteries.

Woman of Honour is a piece set in pace to unravel the hidden cause behind every successful woman in the tale of mankind. Over time, we have seen how many girl children grow up to become a nonentity which is not the original plans of God for their life.

In this series, the potency of feminism will be converse to you. It isn't a book as many would think. Indeed, it's a formula from the Frontiers of Zion set in space to stir up the girls, ladies and women of these last days.

Allow me to bring you the words of a great figure–Edoh Reuben.

"The very moment I place this book on my fingertips, I began to experience reactions of various kinds taking effect in my bloodstream. I felt with within me; I wasn't reading an ordinary book other than the compilation of mysteries!

I came to realize more than I knew to be a woman when I read this book. It channels the distinctive and unrevealed knowledge I've long for throughout the time I've spent in this mortal realm.

When you go through this book, you will come to discover that they are a lot to all you know.

One fascinating thing I find remarkable about this book is that the author communicated it on the platform of Godliness; teaching, revealing, and you know, disclosing the original nature of God to every women, ladies, and even girl child out there. You know what? This edition isn't for feminist alone but all. Too, the men can read it irrespective of the theme.

I love the part where he linked an honourable woman to a medic whose job is to inoculate the virtue of godliness in her children, also act as a missionary that will aid the moves of the end-time revival even to the edge of the Earth. With all due respect to the reader of the very mysteries set in place, I have the desire to make a simple request; tell more out there about this book.

God has sent Stephen on a mission to revamp the lost vibes of feminism back into reality. I'm so proud of his achievement at his young age. Amongst all the books he has written so far, he hasn't done single research. It's a grace espoused mandate!"

Thank you.

Edoh Reuben.

The Chronicles Of Love

THE CHRONICLES OF LOVE is narrative nonfiction and a stimulating edition of love tales. It was set in place to convey a striking message of love to every teenager, bachelor, spinster, and even couples of all ages. Unfortunately, many people have overtime given a wrong interpretation of the term love. Love is an action that split forth a decent aura in its region of orchestration. It transpires from the feeling that a virtuous character espouses. The effects, love transpire provides an individual with a quantum lift. Besides, not just an individual alone benefit from love. Nations to do. In this edition, you'll be sailing across thrilling tales that will entrust you with a quantum lift. A good number of them, includes The Andibilia's Tale, Couples and Newborns, Don't slip away, Delilah the Barber, and the host of other interesting tales. This isn't just tales but sets of inspiring mysteries set in space for your uplift. Love isn't just a feeling as many individuals felt. It is a reality. Everyone wants to be loved, appreciated and you know, cared for. But the question here is this: how many truly understand what the term love details? For this reason, this book was set in space for your uplift. It is time to skip being a mediocre. Common, click on the link, get a copy of this edition, and begin your adventure of ecstasy.

The Wolf God

Gods of Bronze

Prequel Novella

Perseyus
and the Serpent Demon

DAN DAVIS

The Wolf God

Copyright © 2020 by Dan Davis

For information contact:
dandaviswrites@outlook.com

ISBN: 9798645265083
First Edition: May 2020

1

The God

Perseyus stood at the mouth of the cave, his god-gifted flint spearhead dripping with the blood of the demon's acolytes. The corpses of those acolytes lay further down the mountain, along with the bodies of his fallen men, all slain in the sudden battle to reach the lair of the *yotunan*.

Thousands of bones from men and women and cattle and sheep littered the mountainside, some bleached white with age and others yet shrouded in rotting flesh. Perseyus gripped his spear tight and peered into the darkness before him. The cave entrance was low and wide, like

the mouth of a serpent and the stench of death boiled forth.

It was half a year since the day the wolf god had appeared on the horizon and commanded Perseyus to slay the serpent demon. Half a year of travelling south with his men across the plains and into the mountains between the two seas, through the territories of fifty clans and into lands where the men lived in villages in all seasons and built houses of timber and grew fields of emmer and millet. Those villages did homage to the demon by their endless offerings of cattle, bread, and human blood.

Blood was why Perseyus had come but now that he found himself at the final step, it was as though his feet had turned to stone.

He glanced over his shoulder at the sun hidden behind the white clouds that boiled from the mountains below the roof of the shining sky. The clouds had been white and the sky blue that day in early spring on the plains when the wolf god had come for him.

He recalled how the wagons had been

creaking and the oxen that pulled them snorting and shaking their heads after the long day's journey. Perseyus had been out ahead of his clan on foot, wondering whether to order them to make camp on the grassland for the night or to push on for the valley he knew was ahead when his men had whistled a warning.

Grasping his war axe, he had turned to look to the north.

In the distance, a tall figure had approached at a walk, striding forward with a long gait, a spear in hand, and two dogs at his heels.

"Bring up the clan," Perseyus had commanded. "We must protect them."

His companions looked at him. "It is but one man, lord."

"Keep the women together between the wagons and bring the cattle in close. Keep watch in every direction."

They nodded, understanding that much, at least.

His closest companion, Uksen, hefted his stone hammer onto his shoulder. "You think we

will be attacked by this man's clan? Might be they lie beyond the rise there. Or there." He pointed to the horizon.

Perseyus did not know what he thought but he felt uneasy. No man wandered the plains alone, not even with dogs at his side. A koryos of raiders would be three young men at least and more likely nine or twelve. And there was something about the way the distant figure walked...

"We must be ready for whatever comes," he said, sending them to their tasks.

The clan was soon gathered between a rough circle of wagons and the women and children were within. His men stood ready with their flint tipped spears, bows, javelins, and polished stone war axes and fighting hammers at the outer edges, looking all around and listening for the sound of approaching men or horses on the wind. Perseyus stood a bowshot away from the rest of the clan with his eleven best men behind him to wait for the approaching figure.

As he drew closer, Perseyus' unease only

grew. The man was tall but it increasingly seemed he was unnaturally so and the dogs beside him, he soon realised, were not dogs but wolves. It was not unknown for wolf cubs to be raised by a clan but they were unruly and fought always with the dogs and most were culled and skinned in their first year. His own dogs barked furiously at the approaching wolves and the tall stranger and could not be silenced, though the herders shouted and beat them with their staffs.

"Perseyus," Uksen said, staring at the man. "Something is wrong." Uksen was built like a bull and feared nothing on earth but even he sounded nervous.

"All will be well," Perseyus replied, without taking his eyes from the approaching giant. "Stand ready."

"Should we shoot him, lord?" another companion asked, brandishing one of his javelins.

"Master your fear," Perseyus snapped, though his own heart raced at the sight of the figure.

He was thin, with long arms and legs, and his hood and cloak were wolf fur, like those worn by a koryos, and his clothes beneath were likewise grey. The hood was pulled down low over his face but he had a long grey beard that blew sideways in the relentless wind. In his fist, the spear shaft was thick and taller than the top of the man's head with an enormous flint blade shaped like some great leaf.

"Is it him?" Uksen asked, his voice cracking.

Perseyus said nothing but dried his hands on his cloak and tightened the grip on his war axe.

When the tall man was within long spear throw range, he looked up at them from beneath his wolf hood.

He had just one eye.

All knew in that moment that they were looking upon the mighty Kolnos, the wolf god, lord of wisdom and song. It was too much for Perseyus' men and they dropped to their knees and bowed their heads, reciting the sacred words under their breath.

Perseyus forced himself to remain standing

and held ready his war axe as the god came to a stop before him. The wolves stared with their mouths open and their tongues hanging out, panting. Perseyus was the tallest man in his clan, and in all the clans he had encountered in his life, but the god was more than a head taller than that.

"You are the one who is godborn," the wolf god said, his voice as deep as thunder.

He could resist the god's power no longer and he dropped to one knee, bowing his head. "Yes, lord. I am Perseyus, a son of the Sky Father."

"Then I have found you at last. That is well." After a moment, Kolnos cleared his throat and Perseyus looked up to see the god's single eye twinkling. "You will now offer me hospitality, young Perseyus."

Perseyus swallowed before answering. "At once, lord."

Kolnos stood alone with his wolves while the tents were erected and Perseyus stood nearby, watching his people work swiftly despite their

awe at the visitation. None of them had ever seen a god before, though all knew of tales of such visitations. Indeed, Perseyus had been conceived when the highest of all gods had come down from his mountain and all knew of that story. His own tent was built first and soon Perseyus invited the god within. The two great wolves sat outside beside the entrance, watching the rest of the clan and licking their lips at the cattle and sheep.

The god stooped even at the highest point of the tent. Perseyus offered his own low stool in the place of honour, which the god accepted, though it sank into the ground even through the thick furs, felt and leather that made the floor. Sitting to the god's right, in the guest place in his own tent, Perseyus was silent while the women built a fire in the hearth. They fumbled their work due to their shaking hands but the god did not appear impatient. Indeed, he had a smile beneath his beard as the flames devoured the wood. The god then drank off three cups of milk and ate a whole new cheese even before he

started tearing into a cold leg of roasted lamb.

It was astonishing to Perseyus that the immortal Kolnos was so like a man. He ate and breathed, he reeked of sweat and of wolves, he even belched and broke wind and did so with evident satisfaction. Some said that when they descended the mountains to come to the forests and plains of earth the gods took on mortal form as a man might wear a cloak and was otherwise a being of shining spirit. But others claimed the gods were mighty giants who could either see beyond every horizon at once and climb with ease above the sky or shrink themselves to the height of a man as they needed. Whatever was the right of it, Perseyus found it difficult to imagine the stinking, belching figure before him transforming into a shining spirit of the night and of the wolf and filling the hearts of men as they sang the songs of their ancestors. But he supposed it had to be true.

"You bring prosperity to your clan," the god said with a sigh of contentment, cuffing his

mouth as he tossed the bone to the feet of one of the women. "Feed my wolves," he commanded and she snatched it and went out in a rush. "You also," he said to the others and all the women went out, leaving Perseyus alone with the god.

"I am indeed blessed with prosperity, lord," Perseyus said.

"But no horses," the god said, peering down with his single bright blue eye.

"We had some but they died. I will take more now that spring has come."

"I had hoped you would have horses." The god nodded slowly. "I had to eat mine this winter. You should find horses for your journey, godborn."

Perseyus sensed something more was being said. "My journey to the summer pastures? We are almost there, though we shall have to fight for our place and drive other clans away."

"Not the summer pastures." Kolnos' eye twinkled. "I meant your journey to the lair of the demon."

Perseyus shook his head. "I do not understand, lord."

The god picked at a piece of flesh in his teeth, rolled it between his fingers and flicked it into the fire. His hands were huge and strong and looked capable of crushing a man's skull. "You have sons?"

Gritting his teeth, Perseyus forced himself to hold the god's gaze. "My wife could not bring forth the child. Both died."

The god narrowed his eye and when he spoke it was a low rumble. "How many years have you?"

"Twenty-three."

"Ah," he said, his eyebrows arching. "You are but a cub yourself. Plenty of life in your loins yet. Do you know the godborn do not age as other mortals do?"

Perseyus' heart raced to be conversing with a god and to be speaking so openly about sacred knowledge. Kolnos had grey hair and a long grey beard but the skin beneath hardly bore a wrinkle and it was unblemished. Indeed, it almost

glowed with good health and youthful vigour. The only fault to be found was his missing eye.

"I have heard it said that the godborn will never grow old," Perseyus said. "Yet none of my people have seen any godborn but me and there is nothing in the lore. And as for aging, all I know for certain is that I grew to manhood in the normal manner, alongside the other boys of the clan."

The god wiped the corners of his mouth with a knuckle before he spoke. "You became a man. But now your ageing shall slow such that to mortals you shall seem to be as ageless as a god."

"But the godborn are mortals, not gods."

"You are not a god, that is certain. Your mother was mortal and so you will never be admitted to the mountains of the gods. The godborn are of the dying ones, not the deathless ones. But the godborn are not entirely mortal either." He leaned forward. "You belong nowhere, Perseyus."

Perseyus frowned. "Lord, I belong here. I fought with my koryos to gather wealth and

strength. We took control of this clan and now it is mine." He looked at the entrance of the tent. "It is mine," he added.

For a moment, it seemed as though the god was angered but then his eyes wrinkled in the corners and he smiled. "Your people do not fear you?"

Perseyus looked back at the god and wondered at the question. "They fear me enough."

Kolnos nodded slowly. "How long, I wonder, before they turn against you? I have seen it before, in other mortals who were born from a god. You know, Perseyus, just as the godborn are difficult to bring forth, it is often difficult for a godborn himself to father a child. The children grow too big, too strong. Only the strongest of women can carry one and even then the might of the infant in her belly can kill her before the end."

"I find your words to match my experience, lord."

"Not many godborn walking the earth,

either," the god said, winking. "You may be the only one alive today fathered by the Sky Father."

Confused, Perseyus lifted his head. "You do not know, lord?"

The god spread his arms and shrugged. "There may be others, of course, passed beyond my knowing. Where the Sky Father goes and what women he finds, even I cannot follow. The poor girls, like your mother, who suffer his attentions, so often die as their belly swells beyond the strength of their body." His eye narrowed. "He is terrible, you know. Terrible. Feared by all, even the other gods."

Perseyus stared, astonished. "You fear him, lord?"

The wolf god scoffed and then looked closely at him. "You understand, Perseyus, that my words are meant for you alone. As one who is godborn, you are something like a nephew to me." He paused. "Or a young cousin from a distant clan, perhaps. You must know that never would I speak with an ordinary mortal in this manner. And never shall you repeat my words

to any mortal as long as you live. You understand?"

"I do and I am honoured, lord."

The god stared for a long moment before nodding once. "Well then, I do not mind admitting to you that certainly I fear him. He is the strongest by far of the deathless ones and the most cunning, despite what is said about me. Oh, I am wiser than any mortal who will ever live and know more than most gods ever will but he who is highest is ever a mystery to me. Why does he take these women? Women like your mother." The god leaned forward and lowered his voice. "Did she ever tell you what happened when he came to her?"

His mother had never spoken of it but somehow he had heard the story, assembled from overheard whispers and the jeers of other children. His mother had not long passed into womanhood and was yet unwedded, when the god had come out of the trees on the opposite bank of the river while the women were collecting water one morning. While they had

bowed in terror at his presence, he had crossed and carried her away into the trees. From the moment she returned to the clan, she had been both blessed and cursed. No great chief had wanted her as a wife for himself or his sons, especially as Perseyus grew into the strongest and best youth of his generation. Without a mortal father to guide him, everything that Perseyus had won in his life had come from his own efforts, including the establishment of his own clan.

Grinding his teeth, Perseyus shook his head before answering. "My mother never told me what happened that day."

The god peered down, narrowing his eye. "You have hatred for him?"

Perseyus recoiled. "He is the Sky Father. And he is my own father. No man is permitted to hate his father unless he has shamed the clan."

For some reason, his answer did not seem to satisfy the god and Kolnos made a low sound in the back of his throat like the warning growling of a great wolf. "Do you wish to know what I

think? I think that the lord of the deathless ones takes mortal women here and there because he knows that while most will die the strongest of them will bear the godborn. That is his purpose. And do you know why he wants to make godborn?"

Perseyus had thought about this all his life. "To make his people stronger. To lead them."

The god sat up straighter and stroked his beard as he nodded. "That is also what I believe. But there is another reason. Do you know where the gods live?"

Everyone knew that. "In the north, beyond the forests, in the mountains of the gods."

"And why do we live there?"

Perseyus did not understand the question. "It is... where the gods live."

"Some like it there because it is cold. They like the cold, it reminds them of the days of creation. Most like the mountains as each god can have his or her own hill or vale or cave." The wolf god paused. "And the gods live in the mountains because that is where we guard the

demons."

Perseyus shivered despite the warmth of the fire. "The demons, lord?"

"They are kept in their caves and in their high valleys where we can watch them. They are evil, you know, and evil must be watched. Guarded and warded. Do you know what the demons are?"

"They are the enemies of the gods."

The god smiled. "You learnt the lore well. Tell me, have you heard of the yotunan?"

"No, lord."

"That is good, I am glad you have not. The yotunan are also called the devourers, or the insatiable ones."

"And they are demons, lord?"

"The enemies of the gods, yes they are. What about the dura, have you heard of that kind of demon?"

"No, lord."

"It is well. The dura are called the destroyers, or the mighty ones."

"It seems there are many kinds of demon,

lord."

"There are many names for them, yes, though what are these but words? In some ways, each is one of a kind but all are committed to chaos and all wish to destroy not only the gods but all the earth. Which is why they are guarded, as are their foul beasts and their mad followers. And yet, every once in a while, a demon escapes and preys on the world of men."

Perseyus nodded as he listened. There were many such stories and he had heard them since he was a boy.

The god stroked his beard as he regarded Perseyus. "It was perhaps thirty years before this one that the Sky Father left his mountain and came down into the plains. He wandered here and there, as he does. I heard he went west to the end of the world to look upon the wild ocean and then to the east across the grasslands to the mountains of the horse hunters. And in time he came here and fathered you on your mother. But soon after he left his mountain, one of the demons abandoned her sisters and

made her escape to the south. She fled quickly and quietly and was lost before the gods knew she was gone. But word reached me. She found a home in the mountains between the two seas and there she preys on the people of those lands. She demands sacrifices be made to her and the clans are raiding ever deeper into the plains to capture ever more cattle and people. She must be stopped."

The god finished speaking and stared at Perseyus.

"You are going south to slay the demon," Perseyus said, finally.

"No," Kolnos replied, lowering his head. "You are."

Perseyus thought he had misheard. "But you are a god."

"And you are godborn."

"I am mortal, no matter who my father was. If she makes such chaos upon the earth, why do you not kill her yourself?" As soon as he spoke, he knew he had erred and when the god replied, his voice was low and dangerous.

"I have been generous with you, godborn. Granted you the gifts of my presence and my wisdom." The god stared, his eye reflecting the fire. "If I chose, I could kill you and all your people with ease."

Perseyus' hand darted for the knife in his belt but he controlled himself and bowed his head. "Forgive me, lord. I apologise for offending you."

"You have a little of your father's belligerence in you, I see. Perhaps more than a little." The god grunted. "But that is good. I have no need for a meek demon slayer. It will be a dangerous task."

"It is your will that I slay the demon," Perseyus said, speaking slowly. "Even though I may fail where a god would be certain of victory?"

"You see, son, I could kill your whole clan and none of the gods would be offended but I cannot kill a demon. It is not permitted."

Perseyus could understand that there were rules even for gods. "But why does the Sky

Father not take the demon back to her cave and guard her once more?"

"Because he has you."

His heart began to race, sensing that he was trapped. "I have a clan to protect."

"This is the best way to protect them."

Perseyus shook his head. "They will be lost without me."

"This is not how a man accepts the commands of a god. You must do as I command with all the strength of your body and spirit together. To do anything else is to invite only death."

"Once again, lord, I beg forgiveness."

The wolf god sighed. "What do you want for your life, Perseyus?"

"Lord?"

"What is it that you desire?"

"I have won much of what I once desired, lord, and now I wish only to take a good wife, to father strong sons and daughters, and to win undying glory through my deeds."

"Ah, yes, the path of men," the god said,

smiling and nodding slowly. "Most men will have his wives, his children, and his tents and wagons and the sons of his sons will remember his name. But you are one of those who wants more. It is your nature to seek glory above that of all men. So how do you mean to win it?"

Perseyus could see ahead to where the god was leading him but still he answered as if he could not. "To make my clan stronger than all others. To follow the rites, to remember the lore of the clans, and to honour the gods, the ancestors, and the laws of men."

Kolnos smiled and stroked his beard. "You are already wise, young Perseyus and if you hold to the path of men you will be a great chief in your time." He lifted a finger. "But you are only half a man. how many men have slain a demon? You cannot even imagine the glory that will come to you if you walk the god's path. However long you live and wherever you go, you will not live forever and you will not be everywhere. But your name and your deeds may be sung across the earth until its end. A demon slayer would be

known even by the gods." Kolnos leaned forward and winked. "Even by he who is highest."

He had hoped that in time his father would see his deeds upon the plains and hear his name spoken and be proud. But Kolnos was surely right that slaying a demon would bring immediate fame. And of course there was never any question of denying the wolf god's command. Even if Perseyus was godborn, a mortal did not say no to a god and live to brag of it.

"Am I permitted to take my men with me?"

The god nodded. "They are no match for the demon or even her acolytes but of course your men must stand at your side and win their own fame by their deaths."

"These acolytes of the demon, lord. They are not demons themselves and so they are... mortal?"

He wrinkled his nose in disgust. "They are an abomination. Demons bind mortals to them with the power of their own blood. They drink

the blood from her body and they are changed. It causes them to be stronger than mortal men and the blood even heals their wounds, though all this is but an echo of the demon's power. A godborn, if he is strong enough and if he walks the path of the gods, can stand against a demon's acolyte and match his strength. And all your men together may slay one or even two, if their fates allow."

"How many acolytes does she have?"

Kolnos shrugged. "I heard three but who knows?"

Are you not a god? Perseyus thought.

"And what of the demon herself?" he asked. "Is she one of the dura, a destroyer?"

"She is a yotunan, a devourer who thirsts always for blood. Do not think she is therefore some lesser demon, for she is stronger than you and terrible to behold. They call her Medohis, the death serpent."

"This demon is a serpent?"

The wolf god seemed about to answer before he shook his head and suddenly stood. "You

know enough to find her and kill her. Now you will swear yourselves to me. Prepare the sacrifice."

When darkness fell, they were sworn into the service of the god. Perseyus sacrificed the twelve best cattle, one for each of the men of the clan who were leaving their people for the wilderness. They passed from the realm of the clan to the realm of the wild. From the realm of the living to that of the dead. Calling upon their ancestors, they covered their faces with ash, wore their wolf skins, and laid their spears at the feet of the god.

Their wives, children, and relatives stood apart on the other side of the sacred fire, awed by the presence of the god and the importance of the event and terrified at the scale of their loss. The herders and their families stood beyond them with their backs turned so that they would not witness what was not meant for them.

After the god had accepted their devotion, the eleven best men of the clan swore themselves

also to Perseyus and each bound himself with two wide belts of leather that they wrapped around their waists to hold the wolf skins to their backs. Perseyus wore one, as he was sworn solely to the god.

When all were so sworn, Kolnos took his own mighty spear and laid it at Perseyus' feet. The shaft was half as long again as any other spear he had seen and it was twice as thick. The spearhead was enormous and heavy, shaped like an ash leaf and bonded to the shaft with thick cord covered in black pitch.

"A god's weapon for one who is godborn," Kolnos said, solemnly. "The death serpent is stronger than any man or beast you have ever faced and so you shall need a mighty weapon to slay her. Drive it into her heart and into her skull and do not trust that she is dead until you have cut her head from her body."

Perseyus' hands shook as he lifted it and bowed his head in acknowledgement of the gifts of knowledge and power.

Before dawn came, the god was satisfied that

the rites had been properly fulfilled. "Now I go," he said to Perseyus. "The fates shall weave your path but you must walk it well."

They watched him stride away across the plain, his wolves loping behind him.

In their hearts, they wished to say their final farewells to their families and to issue their final commands. Perseyus wished to tell his people that one day he would return to them and would lead them once more, if they could but survive without him until that day.

But each of the twelve in the koryos knew that they had already travelled beyond their people. They were now in the realm of the ancestors and would live like wolves until their oath was fulfilled.

Without looking back, Perseyus led them across the plains to the south toward the lair of the demon Medohis, the death serpent.

2

The Bull

With their wolf skins over their heads and on their backs, they lay in the undergrowth at the edge of a woodland, watching the progress of a strong clan along the river valley beyond. The sky was bright and the sun high over fast clouds, while the wind howled through the trees.

For months they had slipped through the territory of one clan or another, often raiding for what they needed on their way south. Three bands of youths in their own koryos had attempted to clash with them, only to flee before

battle could be joined when the younger ones realised they were facing twelve grown warriors with beards and the weapons of men. It was cowardly of them but Perseyus did not blame them, for he meant to avoid whatever fight he could not win. Which was why he had his men hiding from the powerful clan crossing the valley ahead of their route.

"We should follow them," Uksen said beside him, speaking softly. "And steal their horses."

Perseyus nodded, counting the people and animals of the clan as they walked and rode by. "We shall do it tonight. Though they have many men and their boys will guard the horses."

Uksen scoffed. "Boys' throats are easily cut and their skulls are as soft as fallen apples."

"We will have to take all their horses or none," Perseyus said. "Else they will pursue us endlessly."

Uksen sighed. "What if we creep in closer, into the tents, and kill the chief and his men? Then we take the horses and there is no one to come for us but women, children, and herders."

While Perseyus thought about it, one of his men came rushing up behind him and hissed a warning. "Riders from the west!"

A group of horsemen were riding hard along the valley, closing off the other side of the wood and crying out with whoops and waving their hands. Twenty riders then broke off from the body of the travelling clan and rode fast to close off this side of the woodland.

"We are discovered," Uksen said, shaking his head. "We shall have to fight."

"We shall fall," one of the others said. "Even you cannot defeat so many, Perseyus."

Another of his men edged closer and pointed behind them with his polished stone axe. "Let us cross the river, Perseyus. It can be swum."

Perseyus stood and looked down at his men. "Do you imagine that because we are once more a *koryos* that we must act like boys? Men do not flee. Take up your spears and your hammers, brothers. We shall fight with such fury that they shall flee from us in terror and then we shall go on to do our duty for the god."

Leading them, he strode into the sunlight and stood with the spear of Kolnos at his side as his men stood to his left and to his right.

The approaching horsemen slowed to a stop at the distance of a long spear throw and came forward on foot without their horses. There were twenty-two of them in all and fifteen more picking their way through the woodland at their backs. Perseyus had never been afraid of pain or of death but he did not wish to die before he had accomplished great things as the leader of a mighty clan. Whatever happened, he wished to live so that he might fulfil his duty for the wolf god and return to his people once more. He swore that he would not die in some nameless southern valley.

"If we wish to live to see tomorrow we will have to kill three men each," Uksen said under his breath. "But if you can kill a dozen, brother, then it's only two each for us." He raised an eyebrow. "Shouldn't be too hard for one who is godborn."

"Be silent," Perseyus said, his eyes fixed on

the approaching chief.

The chief wore a boar-tusk helm and boar-tusk armour across his chest beneath his thick cloak. The tusks had been sliced into hard, flat sections then cunningly sewn to leather and there had to have been hundreds of boars slain to make it. From his belt hung a copper axe and a copper dagger. He was a big man with wide shoulders and a massive head beneath that helm but by the size of his gut and his limping gait, it was clear he was an ageing leader. When he came closer still, Perseyus noted the man's grey hairs and the scars on his face and forearms. Old he might be, but he must have been a gifted warrior to have retained such a sizeable and wealthy clan. Even so, there was only one way that Perseyus could imagine him and his men leaving that valley alive.

Stepping forward three paces, Perseyus raised his god-spear over his head and roared the challenge.

All the approaching warriors stopped and looked at their chief.

No leader could refuse such a challenge from a stranger and retain the respect of his clan. The challenger and the chief would have to fight, spear against spear, while their men watched until one was defeated and one was victorious. Not all who lost were slain but a living loss was perhaps a worse fate than death, especially if he was the man who had issued the challenge.

Perseyus knew he could defeat almost any mortal, no matter how experienced and wily they were. The strength and speed given to him by his father the god of the sky had brought him victory thrice before, each time winning to his side a portion of the defeated clan. When he had suffered wounds, those wounds healed swiftly. Terrible wounds might take a day or two to knit together without even leaving a scar but smaller and shallower ones healed even faster than that.

Still, there was not such a vast gulf between him and the very best mortal warriors and a spear thrust to his throat or through his head would surely kill him just as it would kill any

man. And Perseyus suspected that the powerful chief opposite him was one of those very best mortal warriors. His size, his age, his scars and the way he held himself all spoke loudly and Perseyus thought he might be in for the fight of his life.

The men on both sides were silent, watching the two leaders approaching one another. They all knew that their lives would be changed forever if their chief lost the challenge. The losing side might be offered a place with the other clan or they might be allowed to go free. Sometimes, the losers would be killed by the victorious clan or they might choose death over a life without their beloved chief, for the shame of living on beyond the portion allotted to their leader was for some a fate far worse than death.

After staring at each other for some time, the enemy chief slowly removed from his belt his copper axe.

Perseyus readied himself for combat. He knew he could win if the big man fought only with the axe, for the spear of Kolnos was long

indeed.

But the chief dropped his axe at his feet and pulled the copper dagger from his belt before dropping that beside the axe at his feet.

Perheyus knew then that it was to be spear against spear and bent his knees, levelling his weapon at his waist and pulling it back ready for the first thrust which he would deliver after rushing straight at the ageing chief before him.

But the chief then placed his spear on the ground beside him, spearpoint facing away.

He was now unarmed and he stepped forward with his hands spread out to his side.

Perseyus was stunned. The only times he had heard of a chief declining a challenge was when they knew it was their time to step aside for a younger man, oftentimes for their own son. But not only had the chief declined, he was also approaching as if in friendship.

"It is deceit!" Uksen hissed. "Slay him now."

Perseyus could never have done that. Instead, he lay down his own spear in the long grass and walked forward with his arms out beside him

while the men watched them in silence.

"Beware the pack of wolves in the woodland," the old chief said when they drew close, his voice a deep rumble and raspy with age. "That's what my men told me. We thought you were a *koryos* and that we would drive you away. And you wear the wolfskin and the belt, and your hair is unkempt and your beards unshorn. Yet I see you are men grown. One or two men with a *koryos* of youths, I would expect but all of you... what are you? Why are you crossing my valley?"

"We are sworn to the wolf god Kolnos," Perseyus said.

The chief frowned. "You are outcasts? What was your transgression?"

"There was none. The god himself commanded us and we obeyed. We are crossing this valley, heading south into the mountains. That is all."

He narrowed his eyes. "What do you mean, the god commanded you?"

"Just as I say."

Scratching his beard, the chief glanced at his men behind and to both sides of him. "Where is your clan? Are they beyond the river? Over the ridge?"

"We have no clan. We are a *koryos*. I am the *koryonos*."

The chief pursed his lips. "I do not say that you are a liar. But these are bad times and I cannot let you go."

In anger, Perseyus took a step forward and the enemy raised their bows and their spears. "Fight me, then!"

"I have seen one or two men as tall as you in my time," the chief said, his voice level. "But never one who looked so strong or who moved as you do. The strength of your ancestors fills you, I see it. I would fight any man who walks the earth. But there is something wrong with you. And so you will die by the arrow."

As he turned to leave, Perseyus raised his voice. "From this day on, you will live without honour!"

The chief paused and turned back. "I lost my

honour long ago, son. These are bad times. We are all cursed."

"You speak of the demon," Perseyus said, blurting it out. "You speak of Medohis, the death serpent?"

The chief shrugged. "Long ago, I chose to submit rather than die. Killing you will be but little shame when compared to that."

"I go to slay her."

Staring at him and his men for a long moment, the chief slowly nodded his head. "That is why you are a *koryos*? You are going to kill the demon..." Suddenly, he held out his hand, smiling behind his beard. "I am the great Taurohermos. No doubt you have heard of me. I will help you."

Perseyus frowned. The name Taurohermos was familiar but he had not heard the song of his deeds. It was a long way between their clans.

"You will help me?" Perseyus said. "You wish to join my quest to defeat the death serpent?"

Taurohermos glanced at his men and looked back at Perseyus. "I must lead my people, not

run into death like a young man. No, I will not join you. But I will feed you well and send you on your way so that you may do what must be done." Seeing Perseyus' hesitation, the chief rubbed his beard. "Before my men and yours and in view of the gods, I offer you guest friendship." He smiled. "You will find me a generous host."

Perseyus nodded slowly and extended his hand. They shook.

While the great clan made camp in the valley, Uksen stood at Perseyus' side and spoke in his ear. "He is the strangest chief I ever saw. He refused to meet your challenge. Are you certain that we can trust one who has such contempt for the way of men?"

"His offer of guest friendship was spoken before the gods."

"You honour the gods properly, lord, and yet there are men who do not."

"I am no fool, brother," Perseyus snapped. "We will trust him enough to go into his tents and share his food but no more."

Uksen nodded once and placed a hand across his belly. "Good. I'm hungry."

They were welcomed and given meat, milk, and fresh cheese as they sat around the hearth fire in Taurohermos' tent. The chief's men removed his boar-tusk helm and chest armour, placing it reverently at his side, along with the chief's array of weapons. Perseyus had accepted the guest friendship of Taurohermos but still there was something threatening about the way he displayed his weapons. A feast between friends was no place for such posturing. Perseyus attempted to catch the eyes of his men but they were too busy eating and casting looks at the women.

Taurohermos smiled at him and spoke softly. "I see you wear your oaths lightly."

It was a mortal insult and Perseyus threw down his food, ready to jump to his feet. "You will apologise."

The smile on Taurohermos' face wavered. "Oh, you are offended. What a proud one you are. In that case, yes, I will apologise for

offending you, mighty warrior. And yet... no true *koryos* would accept a guest friendship, no? I thought you were wolves."

Perseyus shook his head. "My oath is to slay Medohis. That is all that matters." In truth, his host's words had disturbed him but he pushed the thoughts aside.

"Ah, I see. An oath to a god comes before all else. I understand that completely." Taurohermos smiled again and they continued to eat.

"Your cattle looked fat and you have more than a hundred of them," Perseyus said when he could stomach no more. "Not to mention the sheep and your swift horses. And yet you said these are bad times. Cursed times."

Sitting on the floor of furs, Taurohermos leaned back against his low stool and stared into the fire with a cup in his hand. "The cattle are not mine. Even now, I drive them into her arms."

"The death serpent takes them?"

Taurohermos nodded slowly. "At least, her

acolyte comes to take them, along with a few shepherd boys from the hills, and they drive them into the mountains."

"I do not understand," Perseyus said.

After taking a sip from his cup, Taurohermos sighed. "Many years ago, the demon passed through here. A great serpent, they said she was. Tall as an ash. Vicious. Evil. Men tried to stop her but she killed most of them and the rest fled. Two years after that, her acolytes came. Walking out of the wilderness as if they were men. But they were not men. They demanded an offering from every clan and any who opposed or defied them were slaughtered. My brothers and I attacked them and they killed us all with ease. My legs were broken but I was spared, as were my people, in exchange for the offering. A hundred cattle at the feast of high summer at the mouth of the Valley of the Stones."

Perseyus sat up straighter. "A hundred cattle every year? How do you do it?"

Taurohermos shrugged. "We subjugated the clans. They bring us theirs or we take them. And

if we do not, the acolytes take our sons and our daughters so that the devourer can drink their blood." He handed his cup to a woman, smiling briefly at her as she stepped away. "What would you do, young servant of Kolnos, to protect your people?"

Now Perseyus understood the chaos that the demon had caused and why so many of the clans they had encountered so far on their journey had been so wild. The further south they had travelled, the more dangerous it had become. Young men of the *koryos* roamed the plains and the forests and the clans everywhere were wary of travellers. The normal turning of the world had been knocked out of balance by her endless demand for blood by which she drained the life out of the plains. The lords that had once walked the path of men were descending into the path of beasts.

"And you are now taking this offering to her acolytes?"

Taurohermos scratched at his beard. "To one of them, yes, we are going there now. It has been

the same acolyte for twenty years and he has not aged a day between now and then, while I have become an old man." He made a sign against evil.

"Good," Perseyus said, nodding to himself and smiling. "Very good."

"You cannot do him harm," Taurohermos said, speaking quickly while his eyes grew wider. "We tried once and we failed. We failed terribly. They are stronger than you can imagine."

"So he will not expect to be attacked while he comes to take your cattle. My men will lie in wait and you and your finest warriors will join us."

"If I help you to kill him," Taurohermos said, his expression dark, "the others will come and slaughter my people."

"We shall not kill him," Perseyus said. "At least, not right away."

3

The Acolyte

"This is madness," Uksen said. "I will obey your every word without hesitation but, my brother, you know this is madness. We should just kill him."

"No," Perseyus said.

"When he arrives, we fill him with arrows, throw the javelins and rush from all sides."

"No."

They sat hidden behind a grey boulder on the steep side of the valley where Taurohermos had encamped his clan. Beyond, the green hills

became dark mountains and in the far distance there were some topped with shining snow. Up there, somewhere in that great mountain range, was the lair of the demon. Six days, they had waited for the acolyte to appear. Taurohermos' clan had held their high summer rites down in the valley while Perseyus and his men stayed apart and still the acolyte had not appeared.

"We can find her without him," Uksen said. "Let us kill him when we see him or go on without him."

Perseyus thought that was probably true but there was still so much that he did not know about the demon and her acolytes. How many did she truly have in total and what were their strengths, their powers and what weapons did they carry? The knowledge would help him to defeat the demon, he was sure of that, and then he could get back to his clan. The god had told him that his men would likely be killed but he meant to take as many of them home to the clan as he could. In his imaginings before he fell asleep at night, he dreamed of bringing every

one of his men back to the clan so that they would be as strong as they ever were. With all of his men as well as the tale of his destruction of the demon, clans from the forests to the seas and right across the plains would sing of his name and his deeds. But if he lost all of his men, even reaching his clan let alone taking it back might prove impossible. And who would sing of his fame then, even if he did defeat the demon?

He looked at his friend. "In all our raids we must have taken a hundred men prisoner. You will cease fretting."

Uksen crossed his massive arms. "I'm not fretting. He's no mere man, this acolyte, he has been granted her power, her strength, so why take the risk? And I'm not fretting."

As much as he tried to ignore it, there was another reason for needing to take the man prisoner. He was afraid of the demon. Not afraid of death, for he had faced that countless times and he had never flinched. But he thought endlessly of failure. Of failing to slay the demon. Of facing her and not being strong enough to

bring about her defeat. Not only would he win no fame, he would die forgotten. A shameful death and a life unsung.

And if he could not so much as capture one of her acolytes, how could he ever hope to kill the demon herself?

"You have my answer," he said to Uksen.

They sat while the sun rode high across the sky and then, from upwind, came the distinctive trill of a bushchat. It was a signal they had used since they were boys. Perseyus and Uksen grasped their spears and looked up the hill to the man who had whistled. Moving his hand slowly, he made the sign that said an enemy approached.

After waiting for as long as he could bear, Perseyus carefully moved sideways to peer down the slope into the rocky valley floor.

A group of underfed boys trudged behind the acolyte as he approached the clan, and Taurohermos hurried to meet him. The chief wore his boar-tusk helm and armour but had left his weapons behind at the tents out of respect.

The acolyte was wrapped in a tattered snakeskin cloak with a close-fitting hood and strode with the steady lope of one who is well used to travelling.

"He doesn't look dangerous," Uksen said. "He's not even that big. Can't see a spear or a hammer or an axe or anything. Let us kill him now."

"We wait until he is leaving with the cattle," Perseyus said. "And we take him. Be sure to bring the rope and make it ready for when—"

Perseyus stopped speaking when he realised that the acolyte was arguing with Taurohermos. Waving his arms and jabbing a finger at his face before turning and looking around at the slopes on either side. Taurohermos lowered his head, as if his helm could protect him from the acolyte's ire.

"What is this?" Uksen muttered.

Perseyus was struck by a realisation. He was so certain of it that it must have been placed into his mind by a god. "We are betrayed."

The acolyte turned back to Taurohermos,

grasped his shoulder with one hand and punched his fist through the chief's chest. He ripped his bloodied hand out, scattering boar tusks at his feet as Taurohermos fell, his empty hands spread wide.

"By the gods!" Uksen shouted.

Perseyus was already moving, bounding downhill, jumping from stone to stone and slipping on the loose soil and scree toward the acolyte in the valley. He glanced up to see Taurohermos' men attacking the acolyte with their spears and hammers. The acolyte ripped a spear from one man's hands, while avoiding the thrusts and swings from others, before using it to strike down the attackers with incredible swiftness, each of his blows killing or maiming terribly. The cattle edged away from the violence and the rising stench of blood until the herd broke, splashing through the stream and pushing against one another as they moaned in fear.

A shout came from behind Perseyus as he ran. Though he did not hear the words, he knew

it would be Uksen telling him to slow down and wait for his men. It was a cry he had heard many times before and Perseyus knew it to be good advice. And yet he wished to reach the acolyte while he was still distracted with his fight against the clan. But the acolyte ripped through a dozen men in as many breaths and when others further away shot at him with their arrows, he raced right at them with a spear in each hand. Thrown javelins missed from close range and the arrows that hit him seemed to do no damage nor even to slow him. The acolyte reached the first of the bowmen and killed one with each thrust or swipe of his spears, twisting and hacking with the speed and fury of a beast.

The men of the clan turned and fled. They ran for their women and their children at the tents, while the herders were already in full flight down the valley, driving away the sheep as they ran.

When it appeared that the acolyte meant to pursue them, Perseyus took a breath as he ran and roared the cry of challenge.

Whipping his head around, the acolyte scowled as he took in the dozen warriors racing toward him across the valley floor before fixing his dark gaze on Perseyus. Beneath the snakeskin, the man was thin but his muscles were deep and hard and he moved like a polecat.

The acolyte pulled back his arm and launched one of his spears. It was a heavy thrusting spear, not made to be thrown at all and it flew faster and farther than Perseyus expected, almost spitting him before he threw himself to the side. The spear hit a stone a few paces behind him with an almighty crack before clattering away and when he looked up the acolyte was racing forward with his second spear in hand.

Perseyus jumped to his feet and raised the spear of Kolnos, ready to fight.

But the acolyte changed direction suddenly and made to run around him.

His *koryos* were now in range. Stones from slings whipped through the air, followed by two arrows and finally a javelin sailed high and fell a

few paces short.

The demon's acolyte ran right at them.

After seeing what the monstrous creature had done to the men of Taurohermos, Perseyus shouted to his own.

"Run!"

But they did not hear him, or their spirits would not allow them to flee in the face of an enemy, and they stood their ground.

And they died.

The acolyte jammed his spear into the guts of the first man and ripped it out and stabbed it through the neck of the second in just a couple of heartbeats. The third rushed in with his club only to be punched to the ground before the acolyte stamped on his head, breaking his skull.

Three of Perseyus' men were dead by the time he reached the acolyte and swung his spear shaft against his back. Such a blow would have cracked a mortal man's ribs and might have split open the skin or even broken his spine. But though the acolyte staggered forward, he turned and attacked at once with his own spear, jabbing

it with short thrusts while Perseyus retreated, blocking with his shaft as well as he could. Never in his life had he faced an opponent so strong or so fast. Even when he faced men with more experience who were expert fighters, Perseyus had always been able to use his strength to defeat them. But now his enemy was as fast as he was and fought with a strength that almost matched his own and it was all Perseyus could do to avoid the incoming jabs as they struck low and high, as swiftly as a viper.

Yet, this was no challenge for clan leadership and his brothers threw themselves at the acolyte all at once, striking him with hammers and cracking stones onto his head and arms and back. Coming in at a run from the flank, Uksen wrapped his arms around the acolyte and tried to drag him to the ground. Though their enemy kept his feet, for just a moment he could not wield his spear and Perseyus jumped forward to smash his spear butt into the acolyte's face, breaking his nose.

They all thought they had him but he got an

arm free and punched one of the men in the neck, crushing his throat and struck another in the head with his elbow, breaking his skull. Enraged, Perseyus kicked the acolyte's legs out and together they brought him down. Perseyus held him while the others tied their ropes around his wrists and ankles and then his knees and elbows and lashed him tight. All the while, he cursed them and spat blood and growled like a beast until Perseyus rained blows into his face. His fists knocked out the monster's teeth, split open his flesh at the eyes and cheeks, and then cracked the bones beneath and Perseyus wanted to crush and pound him to destruction.

"Stop!" Uksen shouted, pulling at Perseyus. "Do not kill him!" Breathing heavily, he pushed Perseyus away from the acolyte. "No, brother, no! Not after we lost so many, master your rage, brother. We have him. It is done."

Perseyus breathed deeply, forcing his anger down. After a moment, he nodded to his friend and saw to his men. All that lived were wounded, with broken fingers or welts or

lesions.

Four were dead and one with a broken skull was bleeding from his ears and groaning. Death would take him soon.

After propping him against a large rock so that he was sitting up, Perseyus slapped the acolyte awake. His dark eyes narrowed as he scowled at them over a large nose and sharp cheekbones.

"You are dead," he said, his voice rasping and his accent strange. "My mistress will devour you, body and spirit, when she discovers what you have dared to do to her devoted—"

Perseyus slapped him across the face with his left hand. The acolyte stared in shock.

"Where is the demon?"

"How dare you call her—"

Perseyus slapped him again. "Answer my questions or I will cut you to pieces."

The acolyte smiled. "I welcome death. I will pass to the other side and serve my mistress forever."

Uksen, standing behind Perseyus with his

arms crossed, scoffed. "Demons have no spirit. And I doubt you have one either. When we kill you, your body will be eaten by vermin and birds. Your spirit goes nowhere."

The acolyte glared from his mask of congealed blood. "Do not call her demon! Your disrespect will be punished, mortals, mark me."

Uksen scoffed again and Perseyus silenced him with a look. "You say she is no demon and yet she terrorises these lands, using you and the others like to you to impose her disorder."

The acolyte stared as if he had been profoundly offended. "Demon, you call her. Fools, you are all fools."

"What is she to you, then? A *yotunan*? A *dura*?"

He gaped. "She is a goddess!"

Perseyus stared back in turn before glancing over his shoulder at his men whose expressions matched his own. "She has driven you mad."

"What else could she be? She came from the mountains of the gods, glorious in her power, mighty and terrible and she chose us to be her

followers." He closed his eyes and whispered. "She grants us a taste of her godly power."

"A taste? So it is true that you drink her blood?"

He eyed them warily. "You are not permitted to know."

"Who are you? You say she chose you and the others? How many of you?"

He smiled, as if recalling a fond memory. "We are of the forests of the north, beyond the plains. Always, my people have lived in the shadow of the mountains of the gods. We live to serve. Our sacrifices go to the gods themselves. When the mistress came, she chose our chief for her consort and us, his brothers of the *tauta* to serve her. Ever since, we have done as commanded by our goddess."

"You terrorise the clans and the folk of the mountains, demanding vast tribute in cattle and blood."

"Sacrifices!" he replied. "All goddesses require sacrifices, even men of the plains know that."

Perseyus shook his head and looked at Uksen, who shrugged. "How many of you acolytes are there? Are there three, as Taurohermos said?"

"Taurohermos..." The acolyte spat another mouthful of blood. "All his life, he was loyal. Until you came."

Perseyus shrugged. "I am loyal to my god."

"As am I!" he spat.

"Loyal to your demon," Perseyus replied. "To a *yotunan*, a devourer."

The acolyte snarled. "I will say no more. You who are impious shall be destroyed. Your only hope is to bow down to her and beg for your—"

Perseyus struck him with a closed fist, snapping his head back and cracking it on the rock then he snatched Uksen's hammer and cracked the acolyte above the ear. He collapsed to one side and for a moment it seemed he was dead and yet they saw him breathing.

"What do you think?" Perseyus asked, standing and looking down on the acolyte.

Uksen sighed. "He is a madman. Either he

was mad when she found him or whatever the demon did to him drove him into madness. He is of no use to us."

"We could force him to lead us to her."

Scowling, Uksen shook his head. "Can't trust him. We'll run down some of those boys he brought to herd the cattle, have them lead us closer. We'll find her without him."

"It would help to know how many more acolytes we might face."

Looking at the bodies of their fallen brothers, Uksen shook his head. "If it's more than one it may as well be a hundred."

Perseyus nodded. "We will bury our men here, take supplies from Taurohermos' camp, and go into the mountains."

He used the god's spear to sacrifice the demon's acolyte, thrusting it through his chest and destroying his heart. Each of his men struck their own blows in turn until the man was no more than a bloody heap of meat and bone.

"In the name of Kolnos, I send your spirit into darkness," Perseyus said. "Your body will

lay unburied to be devoured by the wolf and the buzzard and your passing shall be unmourned and your deeds forever unremembered."

Looking up at the distant peaks, he despaired at ever seeing his people again.

4

The Seeress

Perseyus looked down at the largest, richest settlement he had ever seen or even heard of. The village spread across the mouth of a valley and the sturdy timber houses were thatched with straw. The fields beyond were extensive and there were slopes for grazing sheep. Once, it would have been a prosperous place, blessed with everlasting fertility. But no longer. The fields grew only weeds and the slopes were empty.

He was starving, as were his seven men, after

their long trek through the hills and mountain passes. A handful of boys had guided them until the food ran out and he sent them away back to their people while he went on, following the trail of despair and death until he reached the place he had heard so much about ever since entering the foothills. It was called Ghorda, the home of the greatest clan in the mountains and the king who ruled it was owed fealty by every other between the two seas.

There were no men to greet them as they descended the path into it. No men but a handful of bent backed old men and young boys and even those were outnumbered by the women.

"We are close now to the demon's lair," Uksen said under his breath as they trudged deeper into the village. "She must have killed the menfolk."

Perseyus agreed. "Either the demon consumed them or they fell in war with the other clans. No wonder all we have spoken to knew of this village. Look at it. Look at the

timber. They must all want it. They must have tried to take it."

Uksen nodded. "Even we eight could take it."

Perseyus looked at him. "We shall do them no harm."

"Unless they mean it for us," Uksen replied, looking meaningfully through his eyebrows.

The frightened people led Perseyus and his men to the grandest house of them all, in the place of honour in the centre of the village. The roof was high and the walls strong. Inside, a great fire burned in the central hearth and the hall was big enough to hold fifty cows, Perseyus guessed. Though no animals would have been brought inside such a place, as the floor was made from crushed white stones pounded hard and was swept clean. Even the woodsmoke that filled the air was sweetened by the burning of herbs and fragrant grasses.

Beyond the fire an old woman dressed in white sat being attended by a group of younger women.

"Who is she?" Uksen asked a thin old man with a bad leg. The man was blind but of course he knew who they were asking about.

"The king's mother. The keeper of the fire."

"She is your seeress?"

The old man's cloudy eyes welled with tears as he answered. "She watches over us all. Ghorda would be nothing without her. You must give me your weapons."

With that, he held out a shaking, bony hand.

Uksen raised an eyebrow and with a glance suggested to Perseyus that they could knock down the old man and all the people around them and simply keep their weapons. But Perseyus smiled and shook his head.

"Certainly, good father," Perseyus said, handing over his mighty, god-gifted spear.

The loose skin on the man's arms shook as he took the weapon, almost dropping it before laying it at his feet. "Are you some great *yotunan*, lord, who wields such a weapon?"

Uksen growled at the insult but Perseyus stilled him with a hand, knowing the question

was asked in good humour. "I am godborn," he replied.

Tutting, the old man rolled his blind eyes. "No need to make a jest of me, lord. It is my duty to know."

"But I speak truth, good father."

"I will take your knife, also," the old man said, clicking his fingers as he held out the other hand.

Uksen was offended. "Who are you to take a lord's knife while you question his honour, old man?"

"Honour, is it? Yes, the old and the weak have no honour. I did my duty all my life, fighting at the side of my king and his son. I killed twenty men when my hands were strong and my legs swift and threw myself onto the weapons of my king's enemies but it was not my fate to die a hero and to live forever in song. I was cursed with this portion, cursed with age and weakness, cursed with blindness and still I go on while my great people are worn into nothing. Now, I sing the songs of the ancestors

and I guard the door of my king's mother knowing that none will ever sing of me. Now, brave fellow of the plains, hand over your knives or strike me down with them but tarry no longer."

At that, he clicked his fingers again.

Putting a hand on Uksen's chest, Perseyus did as he was commanded. "We meant no offense, good father, and will not dishonour this hall."

"What is your name, lord?" the blind man said, tilting his head. "I will sing of the day of your coming."

"My name is not yet worthy of being sung," he replied. "Wait outside," he told his men. "But do not go far. And steal nothing from these people. Leave the women alone."

One of his men spat. "Wouldn't touch these bread eaters anyway."

The others agreed. "This place is cursed."

Taking only Uksen, he approached the fire and the old woman dressed in white beyond it. Once, she would have been beautiful and the

remnant of that beauty clung to her like the sage flower that stays in bloom even as the first snows fall to herald winter. She wore a necklace of gold and copper beads with a heavy pendant of turquoise and carnelian below her throat that was the finest object Perseyus had ever seen. Her bench was wide and piled thick with furs and she sat upon it unmoving and with the firelight glittering in her eyes.

"Who are you?" she asked, her voice still strong despite her age but like all the people from the mountains, she was difficult to understand. "What do you want?"

"Only to pass through your valley on the way to the demon's mountain."

She stared at him. "You are taking a sacrifice," she said flatly, assuming that was why they were there. She wrinkled her nose. "You are from the plains, I know it. Cattle, is it? We have none left, now. Nor sheep. Nor crops in the fields. The demon dwells beside our sacred spring and has corrupted its purity. The river flows hardly at all now unless it rains and what

once brought life to this valley now brings nothing but death. Without sheep and cattle, she takes only us, now. But others may pass through with their sacrifices for the death serpent, the blood drinker who is called Medohis."

Perseyus looked around the empty hall. "Is that what happened to your people? She corrupted your waters, you gave all your food to her and now you starve?"

"We have nothing left to give," the king's mother said in her strange accent. "Nothing but our children."

"Your children?" Perseyus asked.

"Ah!" the woman said, sobbing. "The death serpent demands them."

"She drinks their blood?" Perseyus asked.

"She eats them!"

Uksen cursed and made the sign to ward against evil words.

"What happened to your men?" Perseyus asked.

The old woman wept, giving herself up to the

tears. "My son Kwehios, the king, he takes his daughter to the demoness!"

"His own daughter?" Perseyus asked. "But why?"

"She demands it. Her acolyte came and demanded it. The blood of a young woman is sweetest, so they say, and the blood of a king is strongest."

Perseyus shook his head in wonder that any man could do something so shameful and still call himself chief or king. "And the men of King Kwehios accompany him? Is that where they all are?"

"His men, yes. The ones who yet live."

"Tell me, good mother, why did you not send your children away from this place so that they would be safe from Medohis?"

Drying her eyes, the king's mother scowled. "Nowhere is safe. Not with our friends, least of all with our enemies. And beyond it is even worse. All clans raid the others for more women and children to bring to the demoness in place of their own kin." She narrowed her eyes. "From

where have you come?"

"From beyond the hills, far to the north halfway to the forests and the seat of the gods. We come not for your sons and daughters but to slay the death serpent and to return to our own lands."

The mother of the king fed them with goat milk and fresh cheese and with flat cakes of grain cooked on stones beside the fire.

When Uksen grumbled about the lack of meat, Perseyus told him to be silent. "She gives what she has."

"How can we have strength enough to fight without meat?" Uksen muttered.

"If I defeat the demon," Perseyus said to the king's mother, "and if I live to return to my clan, I swear to the gods I shall send to your people fifty cattle and a hundred sheep to repay your generosity."

She leaned from her bench and held out a hand until he slid across so she could reach him. She took his right hand on both of hers. Her skin was dry and thin, over gnarled bones, but

her grip was firm. "I look at you and I believe that if any man can do it, it is you. I think you must have been sent to us by the gods."

He patted the back of her hand. "Only one of them, good mother."

She dropped his hand. "What is your meaning?"

"We are sworn to the wolf god to give our lives to the destruction of the demon."

She held up her hands to the sky and leaned back. "Oh! Oh, how I have sacrificed. So many of our men fallen. And now you are here." She frowned. "How many are you?"

"We are eight, now."

"Eight?" She pressed her thin lips together while she glared. "Eight, you say? But just one of her acolytes can kill eight with a single blow! And she has a consort, a great beast of a man who is the slayer of the sacrificed. Let alone the demoness herself, who is an insatiable *yotunan*. How can you hope for victory with merely eight men?"

Uksen grunted, picking a seed from his teeth.

"War separates the strong from the weak. The heroes from the cowards. We have sworn to give ourselves to this feat. It is the test of fire. The test itself is all, for each man to face the test and to act rightly, to harness his fear and to give up himself to the fire."

The woman's mouth twisted. "So you seek only death"

Uksen sighed and threw down his piece of bread. "We seek only to forget ourselves in the fight, to pass beyond ourselves and into the realm of the gods."

She looked between Uksen and Perseyus. "War is not a woman's business but I have raised five sons and seen them to and from the fire. For some men, their inner beast awakens. But our men fight for the love of their people, their family. I know how in battle men become intoxicated with rage in the same way he becomes intoxicated with love for a woman." She waved a hand in the air. "It is what a man does, what all men do. It is no different from a woman who will throw herself into danger when

her child is at risk. When I was young, I saw my mother's sister throw herself over her son and wrap herself around him while the cattle ran over her. That is what men do in war." She nodded slowly. "And that is what our king, my son, now does for all of us. And you now seek to die for your people, for your lord."

Uksen shook his head, disgusted. "Men do not fight with love in their hearts but with hatred, old woman. With rage. But we are not most men. We are a *koryos*, sworn to the god. Are you not the highest of the women here, the tender of the hearth, a seeress for her people? How can you not understand this?"

She scowled and raised a bony finger to point at Uksen. "I understand all. It is you who are ignorant."

Uksen growled. "She calls us ignorant, lord."

"We are guests here, brother. And remember that they do not know our ways."

"Because they are weak. They have given away their sons and daughters to the demon in exchange for peace. And they are dead anyway.

This is what fighting for love and family brings."

The seeress dragged herself to her feet. "And where are your people? Where are your sons, your daughters? Abandoned, yes? How is it different from what we have done?"

"We fight for the god while you submit to evil!" Uksen said. "There is no sacrifice more pleasing to the gods than to fight and fall on the battlefield. In this life by our lives do we free all peoples of this demon, your people also and then in death we shall go as heroes to the mountain and fight with the gods in the time of the darkening. We will protect our sons and daughters from the afterlife while your men walk like corpses upon the earth."

The seeress made signs in the air and rattled off a curse so rapidly it could not be made out.

Perseyus stepped between them and turned to his friend. "Uksen, wait outside."

For the length of a long breath, he stared, stood and stomped through the doorway. In the silence that followed, the fire crackled and a log split, throwing up a shower of wild sparks.

"You think we do wrong, lord of the plains?" the old woman said, easing herself down again and waving away her attendants. "You think it would be better for our souls for us all to die rather than some of us live?"

Perseyus looked around the great empty hall and up into the darkness of the beams above where the smoke gathered. "There is a path of beasts, a path of man, and a path of the gods. It is proper to walk the path of man."

"You think yourself above us," she said, tilting her head back to peer at him along her nose. "Mortals that think themselves gods are destined for destruction."

"Only those that fail. Some who try the god's path will find victory, and greatness."

The seeress shook her head and pointed to the fire burning in the hearth. "Many men I have blessed from this house before they went off to fight, each thinking he would become great. Mighty. Famed. His song sung by all the sons of his sons. Most came back cold, carried on the crossed spears. Now, I do not doubt your

courage but I fear this will be the portion of life for you and your followers."

Perseyus smiled. "Death in the service of one's lord or one's god is to be mighty. To be famed. All of my men have asked the gods for that very thing and we have all offered sacrifices in the hope that it might be so." He looked down the hall at the entrance where the old man sat shivering on a bench beside the door, his unseeing eyes staring at nothing. "To grow too old to wield a spear is a sadness, no matter how great the deeds of that man's days."

She tilted her head and smiled in turn but it was a bitter smile indeed. "Fine words. Perhaps you even believe them. But when your belly is slit open and your life drains away into the earth, I wonder what you will feel then? Will you be thankful or will you give anything, even your soul, for another day of an ignominious life?"

Perseyus stood and looked down at her. "We shall see."

5

The King

A skinny boy, not yet seven years old, led them along the path through the mountains toward the demon's cave. Most of the route was beside a dry riverbed that trickled here and there with water.

"It must not be drunk, lord," the boy said. "The waters bring death."

Uksen scoffed. "There are dozens of springs feeding this river, they cannot all be corrupted."

The boy shrugged but still none of them drank as they climbed.

"That is her mountain, mighty lord," the boy said at last, pointing with a bony arm at the next peak.

"What about this wider path," Perseyus asked, gesturing at the track that bent away from the demon's mountain. "It looks well-travelled."

The young boy dragged the back of his hand across his nose before answering. "That be south, lord. The route what goes to the lands of the priest-kings."

Perseyus frowned. "You have been there?"

The boy laughed, stupidly. "Only the lords are permitted. Used to be they took all the horses and cattle down that way and the priest-kings give back to our lords shining bronze and things you can't even imagine." He shrugged. "That's what pater used to say, anyway. One time he went down to the land of the rivers, driving the king's own sheep and that's the truth, I swear it. Not no more, though."

"The path is clearly still travelled."

The boy rolled his eyes. "Her acolytes take cattle and horses south now."

"And what do they bring back in return?" Uksen asked.

He shrugged. "Probably blood."

"Very well, lead on," Perseyus said, gesturing at the demon's mountain.

The boy froze, his eyes widening. "It's forbidden to go closer unless you're bringing sacrifices."

"Then you better run on home, lad, before the demon's acolytes catch you."

But the boy did not turn and run. Instead, he looked up at Perseyus, shading his eyes. "I wish you were our king. Old Kwehios wasn't brave enough to kill the demon. He just gave us all up. Gave my sisters up, just like that."

Perseyus slapped the boy on the side of the head. A light cuffing but hard enough to stagger him. "You are the son of a shepherd. Know your place and be loyal to your lord." Softening his tone, he continued. "Besides, mortal men are not strong enough to battle demons."

The boy frowned, rubbing his head. "What are you, then?"

Perseyus looked down at him and thought of his last words to the seeress. *We shall see.* "Go, now, before I make a sacrifice of you myself."

Filled with fear, he stood rooted to the spot.

"Seems he wants to be drowned, lord," Uksen said. "You asking to be drowned, boy?"

At that, he turned and skittered down the mountain back toward Ghorda. Perseyus and Uksen shared a brief smile.

They stood together and looked up across a steep valley to the demon's mountain. The sky was bright overhead but the wind howled and there were no trees, hardly any grass and not even any goats. Just brown and black rock.

"I find myself thinking of my sons," Uksen said, speaking softly. "It is unworthy to hope that I live to see them grow into men but I find myself wishing it all the same." He shook his head at himself. "Do you think the wolf god can see into my heart?"

Perseyus looked at the roof of the world. "Once I thought that the gods could see all in their domains. But ever since I met one I am not

so certain. Kolnos had to ride and walk across the plains before he found me and why would he need to do that if he could see all the earth at once?"

Uksen frowned. "But that's because he had taken earthly form. Now he is a spirit once more, he must be able to see. We are sworn to him."

Perseyus glanced over his shoulder at the others. "I am certain all of us are thinking of our sons and daughters. Even I think about my child who died between the worlds. We will see them again."

"We must not speak of such things, lord," Uksen said, suddenly alarmed. "I am wrong to have such thoughts for that clan is no longer our concern and we cannot hope for the future. That is not the path of the gods but the pleading whine of a herder begging the undying ones for his only ewe to bring forth twins." Perseyus glared at him and he coloured, breaking off.

"All that matters is that we kill her," Perseyus snapped, raising his voice so all his men could

hear.

"You reckon her acolytes are about the hills?" Uksen asked.

"They are probably watching us now."

His men cursed them. "We should have come at night," another said. "Rubbed ash on our faces and crept up in the dark. We are a *koryos* again, are we not?"

"We may be sworn to the wolf god, as we were in our youth, but I say again that we are boys no longer," Perseyus replied and he looked at Uksen. "We shall walk openly to battle, like men and like men we shall meet our fates."

He spoke the truth as each of them had learnt it in their youth and yet they did not like to hear it. Perseyus suspected that they were correct about using stealth and that he had made a terrible mistake. But it was done now and he could not show doubts that would only cause their fear to grow as did his own.

Though he spoke bravely of meeting their fates, all he could think of was being done with his task so that they could make their way back

to the plains. If he wanted the chance to become a great chief then he had to see it done. They had killed one of the acolytes and so he expected two more and perhaps the one they called the demon's consort. Slaying them all and then the death serpent would require all his strength as well as the favour of the gods.

His men looked at him in expectation and Perseyus looked closely at the ground, and at the slopes beyond the gorge and thought he could see a way down and across. The earth was disturbed by the passing of many feet and hooves and some of the footprints were fresh.

"The way is clear," he said. "Come." With that he took the boar tusk helm from its bag over his shoulder and pulled it on. It was fortunate that Taurohermos had had a large head.

"Perhaps there is a better way," Uksen said and pointed out another route with his spear. "We could go around the river and come up in a different place where they do not expect us."

Perseyus looked at him and then at each of

them in turn. "Fear is like fire. A little will warm you but if it is not controlled it will consume you. Hold fast, my brothers, we are almost at the end. We will take the tale of our victory home and our names will be sung across all the world."

Uksen nodded, looking around the brothers of the *koryos*. "Our ancestors are within us. Their eyes are upon us. Let us make our fathers proud."

Perseyus clapped him on the shoulder, grasped the hand of every man one after the other, and then led them toward the demon's cave. They bore nothing now but their clothes, their wolf skins, and the finest weapons they had. Most now carried the copper axes and knives they had taken from the fallen warriors of Taurohermos and so they were as well armed as any warrior could expect to be.

The stench of death was in the wind. Fragments of bone littered the scree of the mountainside as they stomped along the narrow paths between the boulders and tufts of grass. Clouds rushed beneath the blue far overhead

and Perseyus knew that his father, the shining blue sky, was watching him. Would he witness the death of his godborn son, or his triumph over the demon? Perseyus wondered if the gods ever felt pride in their sons or if they were beyond such concerns. Certainly, they desired greatness in all men and in their own sons most of all and so Perseyus meant to win for himself the undying glory that he had always desired. As a slayer of the demon his song alone would bring men to his side and cause lesser chiefs to submit without fighting. As they made their way along the path, with the mountain sloping away to one side and stretching up on the other, Perseyus imagined himself riding a horse at the head of a band of mounted warriors with hundreds of wagons behind them, women with rounded bellies holding hands with strong children, and a thousand cattle and uncounted flocks of sheep stretching beyond every horizon. He smiled to think of it, as if the vision of his portion of life had already come to pass.

The sun was yet high when they came across

Kwehios the king of Ghorda, leading his men back down the mountain. He was a well-made man clothed in furs and brightly dyed wool though he walked with his head bowed and his steps heavy.

King Kwehios' eyes were blank and his dusty cheeks carved with a river of tears when he raised his head to look at Perseyus. His aged face was handsome, though his fine features were filled with despair. The king's men gathered about their lord, protecting him with their bodies and shouting warnings. A few carried sticks and these they brandished while others snatched up rocks in their hands ready to use as weapons.

"Who are you?" the king shouted, shoving his men aside to glare down at Perseyus. "What do you mean by coming here so armed?"

Perseyus waved his own men back and placed his spear on the earth. "I am Perseyus and these are my brothers. We are sworn to the wolf god Kolnos. I have come to slay the *yotunan*, the death serpent named Medohis."

King Kwehios and his men stared for a moment before the faint sound of a woman's scream echoed from the slopes above them.

"Adroma!" the wild-eyed king said. He looked at Perseyus and the *koryos*, took in their stature and bearing and weapons, and turned to his men. "No, no, I cannot. I will not!" With that, he pulled a shining bronze dagger from his belt, grabbed a sturdy staff from one of his men and straightened his back. "With me!"

Leading his men back up the mountainside, the king strode a few paces along the path, slipping in the scree and litter of bleached bones before he froze at the sight of something ahead. His men moved to protect him once more and lifted their weapons.

"They come!" one of the king's men shouted.

From around a bend on the path ahead, eight men clad in snakeskin rushed down with their weapons raised. Some were powerfully built and some were thin but all of them looked like wild men, like men sworn to a god, with uncombed hair and unshorn beards and their

faces were twisted in ecstatic fury

They bore clubs, hammers, and knives and the acolytes of the death serpent fell upon the king and his men like eagles swooping onto calves, crashing into them and throwing them down with the ease of men fighting boys.

Perseyus had been expecting three acolytes and to see eight was a terrible shock. But he did not hesitate.

"Kill them!" Perseyus roared at his men and charged up the slope and into the fray.

Seeing how swiftly the acolytes struck down the king's warriors Perseyus urged his feet on and threw himself into the attack before they reached the king, stabbing at the heart of the nearest acolyte with the spear of Kolnos. The acolyte twisted away from the strike and swung his stone hammer at Perseyus, catching him on the shoulder before he could slow his run. The blow not only sent him sprawling but the pain was terrible. It was worse than being kicked by a horse.

He rolled over and whipped up his spear

shaft into the attacker's knee before he could bring down his hammer on his head. His enemy fell and Perseyus stabbed his spear into the acolyte's neck, ripping it out in a shower of blood. The demon's acolyte grasped the jagged wound where his throat had been as the blood gushed forth and his eyes were yet widened in shock when they rolled back into his head.

Behind him, Perseyus' men threw themselves into the fight but with every moment they were falling to the fury and strength of the demon's acolytes. He grabbed the stone hammer that had been dropped and swung it into the snakeskin hood of the closest enemy, crushing his skull and dropping him before he could kill Uksen.

Stepping to the next, Perseyus swung and struck a blow on the side of his head with such force that the hammer's haft broke, killing him. Three of his men stabbed one of the acolytes and still he killed two mortals with his bare hands before he fell. Perseyus rushed to the next man and speared him in the spine with such force his spearpoint came out through his

stomach, spilling his innards into the dust.

His own men were all dead or dying and the last of the king's men fought to defend him. They too fell in succession as the final three acolytes hacked them down. Perseyus rushed at them up the slope while they were engaged and shouldered one aside before he could kill the king, swung his spear shaft into the chest of the second before bringing down the third with a thrust to the groin. Kwehios crushed the face of the fallen acolyte as Perseyus worked his spearhead through the throat of the man on the ground.

The wind blew through the mountains and the clouds raced overhead. A few men moaned or sobbed as their spirits left them and Perseyus stalked between the fallen acolytes and rammed his spear into the heart or head of each one to be certain they were dead.

All the mortals soon breathed their last. All but Kwehios the king of Ghorda, whose men had died to protect him, and Uksen, who had the strength of an aurochs.

And both Uksen and Kwehios were badly wounded.

"Brother," Perseyus said, kneeling at Uksen's side and dragging him upright against a small boulder.

Blood poured from a wound on his head and one of his legs was twisted and swollen.

"There were more than three after all," Uksen said, attempting to smile. "One got my leg with his hammer." He touched the gash on his head and winced, looking at the blood on his fingers. "Think this was an axe. Did you see how swiftly they moved? Such power. Eight, can you believe it, brother?"

"Eight here and the one we slew before to make nine in all," Perseyus replied, shaking his head.

"All now dead," Uksen said, smiling. "Such glory for us."

"You cannot stand?"

"My leg is smashed and I cannot stand but this axe blow has killed me," Uksen muttered through gritted teeth, his eyes screwed tight. "I

wanted to battle the demon at your side. I failed you."

"We killed her acolytes," Perseyus said. "And now I go to slay the demon."

"Your ancestors go with you," Uksen said, his eyes closed.

"Do not die, brother. We will soon be home with our people. I will bring you to your sons again."

Uksen shook his head as if he was angry but when he tried to speak he mumbled and slumped to the side, his head lolling.

After propping him upright, Perseyus crossed to the king who held a hand across his flank where a spear had cut him to the ribs. Blood ran freely from the side of his head where a gash had cut him and almost severed his ear, which flapped when he moved.

"I sacrificed my daughter." Kwehios stared at Perseyus with an animal wildness in his eyes. "Why did I do that? Why? I must have been mad. And now my men. My village. My dearest Adroma, slaughtered and I did it myself. All

gone. Cowardice and madness."

"Your people will be saved. As will mine." He stood and held his spear upright at his side. "I will kill the demon."

King Kwehios broke off from his rambling. "I think you too must be mad."

"Mad enough to fight a demon," Perseyus said.

"Here!" the king said and lifted his bronze dagger, presenting it to Perseyus.

It was covered in blood and yet still a wonder. The blade was as long as his forearm and was as wide at the base as his open hand, both straight edges meeting in a fine point. He had never seen so much metal nor any so hard or so sharp.

"Take it!" the king said. "Use it to kill the serpent. Free my daughter Adroma."

It had been a long time since the girl had screamed and it was likely she was already dead. Nevertheless, Perseyus took the offered weapon and stood, looking up the mountain.

"King Kwehios, I will free you all."

6

The Demon

Taking up his bloody spear, Perseyus slid the dagger into his belt and climbed the path toward the mouth of the cave. Bones littered the mountainside on either side of the path, crunching underfoot. Bleached skulls stared at him from the pits of their eyes. Here and there, vipers slithered through the remains, sunning themselves. The mountainside was too high and too cold for snakes. He knew they had been attracted to that place by the power of the death serpent, the demon Medohis.

A pool beside the path dripped filthy water into a gulley and he knew at once it was the sacred spring the seeress had spoken of. It was choked with the corpses of human and beast and a thick film covered the water.

The cave mouth yawned ahead of him and he found himself stopping before it as if his legs had decided by themselves to disobey him. Looking around at the skulls and rotting bones and snakes, he was overcome with terror.

Perseyus watched his flint spearhead dripping in the blood of the demon's acolytes. The black cave mouth before him was low and wide, like the mouth of a serpent and the stench of death boiled forth.

From the darkness, a woman sobbed.

The king's daughter was alive.

Levelling his spear, he strode into the cave. His eyes adjusted after a few paces. There was just enough light to see a woman lying upon the floor, her legs bound by rope and tied around a pillar of stone. For a moment, he thought there were a dozen warriors standing before him as if

ready to pounce and he readied himself as his heart raced in his chest. But then he saw that they were not men but lumpen pillars of rock and great shards that jutted from the floor of the cave or hung from the roof.

There were no acolytes to be seen and no demon either and yet there was faint light beyond the pillars, from deep within the cave where it twisted and writhed around a corner.

That light seemed to be growing brighter.

Perseyus stooped to the young woman, who stared at him with wide eyes as she squirmed away across the floor as far as her tether would allow. "You are not one of them. Who are you? What are you doing?"

Staring at her, he shook his head. "I am Perseyus. I have come to rescue you."

She stopped squirming, her eyes shining as she looked at the weapon in his belt. "You killed my father."

"He lives," Perseyus replied, touching the bronze dagger. "And granted me this gift that I might free you. You are Adroma, yes?"

She wanted it to be true, he could tell, but still she shifted away from him. "Where did her acolytes go when they rushed out of here?"

"I have killed them," he said, edging closer. "Now hold still! I shall free you."

Drawing the king's bronze dagger from his belt he bent to the rope that bound her and sawed at the part joining Adroma to the rock. The rope was old but it was thick and well-made and strong enough to restrain an aurochs. Still, the sharp edges of the dagger cut through the strands, wiping away the sticky drying blood so that the blade shone.

A growl from the back of the cave echoed from the walls and the light grew further.

"She comes," the girl said in a low, steady voice and edged away, yanking the rope from his grasp.

"What are you doing?" he cried, grasping it and sawing faster, cutting through threads as the rope wobbled. He was almost through.

"Leave me and kill her," she said, her voice steady though her breath was heavy and she

pulled the rope away once more. "There is no time to free me. Go. Kill her. Quickly!"

Heavy steps sounded and the light of a rush torch filled the cave.

Perseyus was certain that the demon had come.

But it was not her that stepped into view from the depths of the cave.

Holding the torch was a large man, as tall as Perseyus yet broader at the shoulder, with thick and powerful arms and a fat belly. His body was naked but for the white and black symbols drawn across his pale skin. The man's massive head was bald and the symbols covered his scalp and face also. Perseyus knew they were wards that protected him from harm. He even had a few tattooed onto his own skin. But he had also killed men in his youth with similar protections and it was said that the symbols had power only when a god's spirit was with you.

Did it work with demons also? Was the demon deeper within the cave and was her protection extended over the hulking warrior?

The warded man lifted a massive blackwood club in his fist as he lumbered closer, glaring at Perseyus and growling like a bear. The black club was as long as a man and the great head of the weapon was a mass of knots worn smooth with use, reflecting the fire like freshly spilt blood.

"Get back," Perseyus said to the girl and she edged aside as far as she could but her rope leashed her to the column of rock. She tugged on it and he tossed the kings great bronze dagger to her while he hefted his spear and circled away from her, drawing the beast of a man with him.

"Use the blade!" she hissed, kicking it back to him across the floor. "Kill him with it!"

The beast of a man looked at the girl and scowled, stepping toward her and speaking something incomprehensible in a guttural tongue.

"I am Perseyus!" he shouted, taking a step forward, leaving the metal blade where it lay. "Sworn to the wolf god Kolnos, whose spear I wield in his name." At this he raised his weapon,

showing it to his enemy as he sidled away from Adroma. "I come to slay the demon Medohis, the death serpent!"

The warded man turned his head slowly, his mouth hanging open and spittle dripping from the corner of his mouth. The light from the wildly burning torch flickered in his black eyes. They were mindless eyes, like the eyes of a beast, and the sight of them chilled Perseyus' heart. Growling again, the warded man lumbered two more steps, half dragging one foot behind him. Perseyus shortened the grip on his spear, ready to step sideways and drive it into the man's face.

With sudden speed, the monstrous enemy rushed forward and swung his club at Perseyus' head, chopping with it with precision like a warrior using a war axe. Perseyus recoiled and ducked beneath the blow but still it hit the back of his head, shattering the helm and sending boar's tusks clattering from rocks and bone all around. Perseyus fell sprawling, fearing that his skull had been crushed. His vision burst apart into a thousand stars and he tasted fresh blood

and foul dirt. A woman was shouting and feet stomped closer and the gods roared in his ear to get up.

Perseyus ripped off the remnants of the helm and threw himself to the side just as the colossal head of the club slammed into the ground where he had been lying. Spitting the foulness from his lips, he shook his head and looked for his weapon but the rush torch was guttering somewhere on the floor and he could see the god's spear nowhere.

Growling, the warded man rushed him once more but this time Perseyus was ready for his speed and he went forward to meet him, lowering his head like a bull as he charged. Grasping the man about the torso he threw him to the ground. When the warded man fell he bashed the back of his head on a rock, the wet smack echoing from the walls. He bellowed and sobbed, clutching his head like he was an overgrown child in a monster's body. Perseyus snatched the man's club, swung it up and brought it down on his head, silencing his cries.

Once the man slumped to the side, he swung the club again to strike him above the ear, cracking the skull. He hit him a third time and the big skull gave way, collapsing in and spraying blood and brains out over Perseyus' face.

Breathing heavily, Perseyus looked out of the mouth of the cave at the mountains beyond and caught a glimpse of the bright blue sky.

Had his father seen him defeat his opponent, he wondered? Could the god of the sky see beneath the earth?

Adroma screamed and Perseyus started, turning at the sound in time to see the demon striding out of the deep darkness, her face twisted in rage.

Medohis did not have the form of a monstrous snake but that of a woman. Her was hair matted into thick locks beneath a tattered snakeskin hood and an enormous snakeskin cloak flapped behind her to expose her naked, filthy body beneath. She was taller than any mortal upon the earth—as tall as Kolnos, perhaps—but her body was that of a woman all

the same. Her bared breasts were round and high and her face, though deformed with anger, might have been beautiful beneath the filth smeared across it.

Her body was thin but strong and the skin over the muscles of her thighs reflected the half-light as she strode into view with her hands out, grasping, the nails long, sharp and black with filth. Her eyes fixed him with their mad glare and as she ran, she began to shriek in an abominable howl so appallingly loud and unearthly that it was as if his feet had been turned to stone.

A moment before she reached him, he stepped back and swung his club in a wild arc, crashing it against her flank with force enough to kill a mortal man.

It was as though she did not even feel it.

Towering over him, she swung her hand as a man might swat a fly. He turned away but still the blow threw him sprawling into a pile of rotting human and animal flesh and bone. Her long, sharp fingernails had ripped open the skin

of his neck and face and his blood poured forth.

From the other side of the cave, Adroma uttered furious curses as she stretched in the dirt for the bronze dagger, her fingertips brushing the hilt while the tether quivered behind her. The demon whipped her gaze to the sound before striding forward with her snakeskin cloak shimmering in the flames. She trod on the rushlight torch without seeming to notice, putting out the fire and sending the cave into semi-darkness.

Grasping the dagger, Adroma sat up and sawed frantically at the rope binding her legs.

Perseyus had lost his spear and his club but if he looked for them then the girl would be killed. He pulled himself to his feet and rushed the demon with his bare hands, crashing into her waist and wrapping his arms around her to pull her down with him.

Medohis staggered and came to a stop, peering down with a surprise in her hideous eyes that turned swiftly to malevolence. She struck him in the head with a bony elbow and the pain

and the force of the blow weakened his legs so that he would have fallen were it not for his grip on her. Still, he held on and she twisted, elbowing him again and hissing in fury as he tightened his grasp. When still he held on she reached down and pried his hands apart.

Perseyus roared, holding on with everything he had but still she peeled his hands away from her, turned and struck him with a closed fist under the chin. His head snapped back and he wheeled away, grasping at nothing, at anything, and finding he had hold of her snakeskin cloak. It ripped in his hands but he held on to the tatters and pulled. Her cloak and hood were one piece and he grabbed another fistful of cloak and heaved back, his feet scraping on the ground. It yanked her head back and she twisted, enraged, and tore off her hood, sending Perseyus flying onto his back with the whole stinking garment in his hands as she stomped toward him.

The matted locks of her filthy long hair now free seemed to shake as she came forward, her

lips pulled back into a snarl. Her teeth were small and pointed and Perseyus scrambled away in terror, throwing himself behind a pillar of stone and peering in a panic about him looking for the god's spear or the club or even a rock.

She was almost on him as he grabbed the haft of a weapon he saw in the shadows. Relieved, he jumped up and stepped back but the weapon he raised was in fact nothing more than a man's thigh bone with a scrap of rotting flesh at the top. Disgusted, he threw it at her face.

This served only to enrage her further and he ran as she shrieked again and rushed toward him, her long legs catching up with him in two strides as he made to dart around a pillar of stone.

She grabbed his head in her hands and lifted him off his feet and pulled his face into hers. Her claws dug into his scalp, cheeks and neck, gouging pieces out of him as he fought to free himself.

He kicked and struggled, punching her arms and kicking at her body as she brought him to

her but she seemed not to feel any of it. Her breath was beyond foul, it was the reek of death, of disease and rot, and for a moment he thought she was going to kiss him.

Then she sank her sharpened teeth into his face and bit down, ripping his cheek and the flesh over his eye. Those teeth gouged deep, scraping against the bones of his skull as she worked her jaw, sucking at his blood like an infant does to her mother's breast.

Perseyus screamed and jabbed his fingers into her eyes.

She threw him down, one side of his face ripped and chewed and bleeding, and through the pain and tears and blood he saw the demon whip her head around at some sound, her matted locks flying.

It was to be his end. Without a weapon, bleeding and broken as he was, he knew that he was finished. The demon would live on, spreading chaos across the land and his own clan far in the north would soon be engulfed in her madness. He had failed.

But in that moment, he suddenly understood why.

He had sworn himself to Kolnos and had done the god's bidding without question but his sacrifice had never been true. He had sacrificed his position to the god but in his heart he had never stopped believing that it was his. Ever since he had left them on the plain, he had thought of little but getting back to them. To leading them once more.

But that was wrong.

Wanting to live, wanting to regain his life back on the plain, wanting to be chief of his clan were not desires befitting one who walks the path of the gods. On his journey he had been promising to return to do war with clans who had wronged him and had sworn to grant cattle to one who had helped him. Always, his mind had been on living, on some later life that he would lead once his task was done. In his heart, he had sacrificed nothing.

It had led him not to the higher path of the gods but to baseness, even indignity and to

failure.

Finally, he understood that it was not for earthly needs that he did battle but for excellence in the face of divine judgement. Fighting with the hope and expectation that he would live had held him back from greatness. Only by fighting without hindrance would he be sacrificing all. His life or his death were immaterial.

He knew he must get up and fight without regard for his body or for future earthly rewards, for only the undying glory of his spirit had any true meaning.

In that moment of realisation, the cave was suddenly illuminated by the light of the setting sun as it sank into the mouth of the cave. Perseyus winced and looked away from the glare.

And there, just out of reach, his spear glinted in the reflected light.

As he leapt for it, the death serpent whipped about and reached for him, raking her hand down his back and tearing the flesh. Her

massive hand wrapped around his lower leg and she pulled him away, lifting him into the air.

But his hand had reached the shaft of the spear of Kolnos and it came with him as he was lifted off the floor. Twisting in her grasp he whipped the massive spearhead up and into her face. The edge cut her cheek and she screamed and dropped Perseyus. He fell onto his back and she stamped on his chest, cracking his ribs and driving the breath from his body.

He could not throw her off and she bore down harder, suffocating and crushing him.

In a few more heartbeats, he would be dead.

But the demon screeched, in pain and confusion, and took her foot from his chest. She scowled, scraping at her shoulders and her flanks.

Despite his broken ribs, and not pausing to question why she had halted her assault, Perseyus forced himself to his feet and thrust up with his spear, puncturing the demon's naked belly and ripping it out in a shower of dark blood.

He retreated in horror as she rushed at him even as her entrails tumbled from the wound, stepping on them as they slipped out in a squirming mass of foul stinking viscera.

Perseyus planted his feet and thrust the spear up under her chin and into her throat.

That stopped her.

He ripped the spear out sideways, blood gushed forth and the demon fell, writhing and grasping and dragging herself toward him still. In disgust, he speared her neck again and again, stabbing and chopping through skin and flesh and spine. Even after the head was cut off, her mouth and eyes scowled and the enormous body twisted and thrashed on the floor.

It was then that he saw the king's bronze dagger in her back, the blade plunged up to the handle.

Perseyus knew he had not caused that wound. When last he had seen the dagger, the king's daughter had been sawing at her tether with it.

After urgently searching, he found her lying

across the cave amongst the bones and filth with her golden hair spread around her in the last light of the day. Rushing to her side, he brushed the hair from her face and lifted her up. There was a bright red mark on the side of her face and there were cuts upon her brow. But she breathed and coughed into his face as he lay her at the mouth of the cave. When she opened her eyes, she struggled against him in panic.

"The demon is dead," Perseyus said, softly, holding up his hands. "She is dead and you are safe."

Adroma stared at him, frowning. "Who are you?"

He smiled. "My name is Perseyus. You are Adroma, are you not?"

She scowled and pushed him away, struggling to her feet and wavering as she stood. As he reached out to steady her she slapped his hand away. "What happened?" she asked, looking at the body of the warded man and at the foul guts and blood and headless body of the enormous demon.

"You stabbed her with the bronze dagger," Perseyus said. "You could have fled." He pointed at the wound on her face. "You were almost slain. Why did you do that?"

She drew herself up to her full height and lifted her chin. "Why did I do it? Because I am Adroma. I am the daughter of a king."

Despite the filth that covered her dress, her face, and her unkempt hair, she was beautiful. The sunlight behind her shone through her hair and through her white dress. She was tall and her hips were wide and her legs strong.

Exhausted and wounded as he was, he wanted her. And by the way she shone in the sunlight, Perseyus knew that his father approved.

"You look like a goddess," Perseyus said and she was more confused than pleased but she was pleased all the same. "And I owe you my life."

She hesitated and then nodded. "As I owe you mine, Perseyus." Adroma frowned. "You are wounded most terribly."

He touched his face and winced, feeling the

pain from the gouges there, and the ones on his legs and back and the terrible aches and bruises he had taken in all the fights. "I will be healed by tomorrow, Adroma."

"How can that be possible?"

Perseyus smiled to himself as he looked to the sky. "I am godborn."

King Kwehios, her father lived, as did Uksen, though he walked with a limp for the rest of his days. The king wept to see his daughter as they came down the mountainside and recoiled when he saw that Perseyus carried the demon's head by the hair. Together, they limped their way down the mountain and through the passes as night fell until they reached the village.

Perseyus was celebrated as a hero and stayed as a guest in the king's hall. Chiefs from villages and clans all around came to grant him gifts, to hear the tale, and to see the head of the demon. His song was sung by a hundred clans and later by a thousand. Kwehios gifted to him the bronze dagger and Perseyus at once gifted it to Adroma, who refused three times before accepting, to

much cheering and approval.

As for the village and its people, their king had in the end chosen the path of the gods and had won his own undying glory. And so the waters of the sacred spring flowed free once more and prosperity and peace returned to Ghorda and the people became as strong as their fathers.

When Perseyus finally returned to the plains, he did so with a hundred followers, herds of cattle and sheep, and a strong wife in the beautiful and shrewd Adroma. He won back his old clan and united many more under him, becoming the Chief of Chiefs throughout his long life, accepting tribute from the lords of the steppe. By his wisdom did he issue justice and by his strength did he create order.

In time, Perseyus and Adroma had seven sons and two daughters and many of them became leaders of their own clans in the vast plains.

Though he never saw the wolf god again, nor his father, nor any other god, he knew by his

prosperity and fertility that he was in their favour. Such is the way for those who live piously and with courage, and who honour the gods and their glorious ancestors.

The godborn are almost ageless and yet they may be killed. And so it was with Perseyus. Many years after his beloved wife had grown old and died, he fell in battle. In a clash of one great clan against another, he was shot full of arrows, pierced with javelins and cut down as he still fought. A warrior's death, as befitted the demon slayer. His grave was dug where he fell and fifty spears were lain with him, along with bronze daggers and beads of gold. His stallions were slaughtered, and his dogs, and sent with him to the afterlife and a hundred cows were sacrificed for the feast. After the contests and rites were complete, the clans built a mound as high as a hill over his grave so all who saw it would know that the greatest of them lay within. But his spirit, all knew, was feasting forever with his father and the other gods, on the immortal mountain.

The undying fame that god-like Perseyus won was never forgotten.

Many years after his death, a granddaughter of Perseyus bore a son to the Sky Father. This young godborn, a great-grandson of Perseyus, was called upon by the wolf god Kolnos not to slay one demon but many. Demons more terrible and powerful than Medohis ever was.

And the deeds and the legend of this immortal hero, demigod, and monster slayer would in time be greater even than those of his mighty ancestor Perseyus.

This godborn was to be known by many names; Holkis, Herkulos, Perkwunos, Herakles, Perkūnas, Thor, Indra, Hercules, Priskos, and the Ancient One.

And his glory will be sung.

AUTHOR'S NOTE

Thank you for reading this novella set in the world of Gods of Bronze.

The first novel in the series, which begins the legend of the demon slayer Herkuhlos, is called Godborn.

BOOKS BY DAN DAVIS

The IMMORTAL KNIGHT Chronicles
Historical Fantasy

Vampire Crusader
Vampire Outlaw
Vampire Khan
Vampire Knight
Vampire Heretic
Vampire Impaler
Vampire Armada

The GALACTIC ARENA Series
Science fiction

Inhuman Contact
Onca's Duty
Orb Station Zero
Earth Colony Sentinel
Outpost Omega

For a complete and up-to-date list of Dan's available books, visit: **http://dandavisauthor.com/books/**

Printed in Great Britain
by Amazon

16573938R00078

Lightning Source UK Ltd.
Milton Keynes UK
UKHW010624230321
380841UK00001B/59

9 781034 626022